Praise for
Beyo...

"Elizabeth Marek's piercing prose sings an alternately mournful and joyful song as it guides the reader through the complex emotional lives of its beautiful yet wounded characters. Haunting." —Patti Callahan Henry, author of *Losing the Moon*

"A beautifully written, deeply moving novel about loss, love, and redemption. Miranda and Abby are exceptionally believable, real, true characters whose stories depict the extremes to which we will go to avoid pain and then to find wholeness. A lovely read." —Jessica Barksdale Inclán, author of *One Small Thing*

ELIZABETH MAREK

Beyond the Waves

FICTION FOR THE WAY WE LIVE

NAL Accent
Published by New American Library, a division of
Penguin Group (USA) Inc., 375 Hudson Street,
New York, New York 10014, USA
Penguin Group (Canada), 10 Alcorn Avenue, Toronto,
Ontario M4V 3B2, Canada (a division of Pearson Penguin Canada Inc.)
Penguin Books Ltd., 80 Strand, London WC2R 0RL, England
Penguin Ireland, 25 St. Stephen's Green, Dublin 2,
Ireland (a division of Penguin Books Ltd.)
Penguin Group (Australia), 250 Camberwell Road, Camberwell, Victoria 3124,
Australia (a division of Pearson Australia Group Pty. Ltd.)
Penguin Books India Pvt. Ltd., 11 Community Centre, Panchsheel Park,
New Delhi - 110 017, India
Penguin Group (NZ), Cnr Airborne and Rosedale Roads, Albany,
Auckland 1310, New Zealand (a division of Pearson New Zealand Ltd.)
Penguin Books (South Africa) (Pty.) Ltd., 24 Sturdee Avenue,
Rosebank, Johannesburg 2196, South Africa

Penguin Books Ltd, Registered Offices:
80 Strand, London WC2R 0RL, England

First published by NAL Accent, an imprint of New American Library,
a division of Penguin Group (USA) Inc.

First Printing, November 2004
10 9 8 7 6 5 4 3 2 1

FICTION FOR THE WAY WE LIVE
REGISTERED TRADEMARK—MARCA REGISTRADA

LIBRARY OF CONGRESS CATALOGING-IN-PUBLICATION DATA:

Marek, Elizabeth.
    Beyond the waves / Elizabeth Marek.
        p.   cm.
    ISBN 0-451-21357-2 (trade pbk.)
    1. Psychotherapist and patient—Fiction. 2. Women psychologists—Fiction. 3. Loss (Psychology)—
Fiction. 4. Mute persons—Fiction. 5. Girls—Fiction. I. Title.
PS3613.A739B495   2004
813'.6—dc22   2004009243

Set in Bembo
Designed by Ginger Legato

Printed in the United States of America

To Marc,
Adam, and Emily

Rich harbor . . .

Acknowledgments

Bringing this book to fruition took more than ten years, and the help of many people along the way. Thanks to Richard Marek and Dalma Heyn for their perceptive (if often contradictory) comments, to my husband, Marc, for his sound editing advice, and to my children, Adam and Emily, for playing by themselves sometimes so I could write. But none of the above would have mattered if not for the wisdom, caring, and nagging of Tracy Bernstein, my editor and friend. Green are the leaves, compadre. There are no other words.

Chapter One

Miranda locks the door behind him. As always, she hears the house settle into silence around her. It holds her like water as she drifts back into her bedroom, parts for her at her touch. She feels her hair flap against her back and she shakes it in front of her face until it touches the edges of her eyes and the wall is gone, and she can see only her hair. It is time to look at her toes.

She sits on her flowered bedspread and takes off her socks. They are still there. She holds each one in her hand and twists them gently back and forth. *This little piggie went to market. This little piggie stayed home.* Carefully she cleans the dirt from around the nails. She pinches her little toe between her fingers and smiles because it hurts her. She smiles again as she bends her big toe inward. By her look alone she can make it do her bidding. It. Him. He is the king, bending to her will. The queen and the little ones move together. It does not please her, and she practices moving them one by one.

She sits on her bed for an hour, and then undresses for

her shower, hanging her robe in the closet. The water is hers. Sometimes there are snakes that rain from the silver showerhead, but today it is the jungle and the water is warm. The soap, white and small, is an animal that spends itself upon her. It rubs its body over her arms and under her arms where hair is beginning to grow. It slips over her chest, and she rubs hard against the swollen parts around her nipples. Soon, her father says, she will grow breasts. That will not be good, he says, because they will have to get curtains. She is sorry because it is her fault. Around and around she moves the soap. She knows that it gives up its life in her service and she thanks it. The shampoo comes out of a bottle and her father buys it at the store.

After her shower, it is time to do her math. She goes to the table, where her father laid it out for her the night before. She loves math. Over and over she does the problems. Four hundred eighty divided by eighty equals six. The square root of six thousand four hundred is eighty. Forever and ever. She is like God, dividing and making whole again. She does all of the problems and then stares at the page. There is eleven, the father, tall and proud, and one, the son. Eleven and one, and they will always be that way. They will never grow breasts or bellies, never need curtains on the windows. Her eyes move down the page to the number six, and it laughs at her. Four hundred twenty divided by seventy equals six. She had been wrong to think the number was in her power. She hears it laughing at her. Frightened, she scribbles over it with her pencil, but the laughter goes on. It is hiding under the darkness she has made, and she rubs at it with the eraser until the paper rips. Now her father will be angry. Stupid girl! Shaking, she gets up from the table. It is a test. Big girls don't cry. Her father says fix it now, now, not later. Her hands are shaking as she copies the numbers onto a fresh piece of paper, saving the six for last, but the six is quiet now and she is safe. When she is done, she puts the paper in her folder. It is eleven o'clock, and time for recess.

From the refrigerator, she gets a glass of milk. Her father has left her a banana. She does not like bananas because they are long and thin, like snakes. Snakes can bite you, and their bite can kill. She holds the banana in her hand, rubbing it. The yellow skin feels cool and smooth. She will eat it, to please her father. It is good to please her father. When she is good, he makes the sun shine for her outside her window. It rains when she is bad. His tears are the rain; when she is bad she makes him cry. Sometimes she does not know what she has done. *You must think about it,* her father says. *It is your job to know.*

She can feel her father's love when he says that he will keep her safe. Outside, there are men with snakes that bite, snakes that spit white venom and live on the blood of little girls. She is her father's little girl. She locks the door after him in the morning and does not open it until he comes home again at night. He once tore off a butterfly's wings and left them on her pillow. It was the day she said she wanted to go to school, and she knew that he was telling her, because he loved her so much, the things that can happen to beautiful creatures in the world outside. *You are a beautiful creature, too,* he said.

After her snack, she does the other work her father

leaves for her. There is English, history, geography. For history, she reads about her city, New York, when it was just a baby, when it was New Amsterdam and little girls could go out on the streets. They wore wooden shoes so the snakes would not bite them. She is glad she did not live in the olden days, because she would have been afraid. There are pictures in the book of monsters with huge wooden faces and no eyes but four long arms that spin and slice up anyone who gets too near. There are walls that hold back the monsters in the sea, but the walls look small and weak. The children are screaming, because they have to go outside. She knows that it is better to live now, when she has a father who can understand why she needs to be indoors, who will let her stay inside and will provide for her. She reads in the textbook that her father has brought home from the school, and writes answers to the questions he has left. It feels nice to write each letter, to look at each word as a family of letters, big and small, mother and father. She writes carefully, especially when she has to write an *s,* so that the letters stay small and safe. When she is done, she reads the parts of the newspaper that her father has marked for her. She needs to learn her current events. At night, over dinner, he likes to ask her about the wars, the fires, the murders, the rapes. She will need to know about each one.

When she gets hungry, she eats the sandwich her father has left her. She presses the bread and peanut butter against the roof of her mouth until it is soft, and then she swallows it. She listens to the noises outside. A siren screams past her window, but she is safe. Because she feels safe, she likes to listen to the cars. Voices come into her ear from the street and she likes them, because she cannot hear the words. The noises are like a river and she floats on it, past days and pictures in her mind of children on swings and dogs chewing on their leashes in Central Park. They carry her outside to a sunny day and the smell of applesauce and flies that buzz around her but do not bite. Her father holds her in the water, which is cool and flowing fast, and she is scared but he says that he will not let her go. The peanut butter is sweet, and when she is done she has apple juice and two cookies. She washes her dishes and puts them in the drain board. It is one o'clock, and she is done with school for the day.

The afternoons are hers, to do with as she likes. All work and no play makes Miranda a dull girl, her father says. She goes into her room and lies on her bed, looking across at the shelves. She has dolls and soft, plush animals that her father has given her. On the shelf below are her jacks, her paper dolls, her markers and paints. She likes to paint pictures of the world outside. Even the snakes, with long teeth dripping clear red blood. But she does not feel like painting now. She closes her eyes and watches the orange lights that dance on her closed lids. Suddenly, she knows that she is blind. She is out of her room, alone in the desert, lost, and afraid, and there is no one to save her.

She opens her eyes and the room is back and she is in it. She laughs, stands up, and goes to the window. Sometimes, she likes to sit at the window and watch the people walk by on the street far below. She can see the children holding their mothers' hands, or being pushed before them in strollers. Her own mother went out through the door one day when Miranda was a little child, and she never came back. *She is dead,* her father said, and Miranda knows that it was the men with snakes that killed her.

Her mother was bad because she went when her father said no, and *Look,* said her father, *look what happened to her.* He would not let her cry, because her mother had been bad, and it was wrong to cry for bad people. It was good that she had gone, and good that Miranda was still safe with him. Her mother had soft skin and smelled like apples. She was the bravest person Miranda ever knew, brave enough to go outside with Miranda's hand in hers, brave enough to laugh when Miranda swung from the monkey bars in the playground, brave enough, once, to yell at Miranda's father *Youshutupyoushutupyoushutupyoushutup. But they got her in the end,* her father said. Miranda might have been frightened, but her father held her close and said that they would never, never get her. Her father's skin is rough and smells like ashes. She does not miss her mother and does not remember her mother. She does not have a mother and did not have a mother and she never had a mother and the woman was a bad woman and was not her mother, and people do not need mothers because mothers go away. Miranda loves her father.

She goes to the mirror and looks at herself for a long time. Her face is thin and pale, framed by long, straight, dark, heavy hair. Laughing, she shakes her head from side to side until her hair lies like a curtain all around her head. She can disappear inside it like an ant in the shag of her carpet and be safe, seeing out while no one can see in. Carefully, she unfurls her tongue and draws a strand of hair into her mouth to suck. *You are a pretty girl*, she hears her father say. *Bad things can happen to pretty girls in this world, Miranda. You just remember that.*

It is almost five o'clock. Her father will be home soon. She likes to hear the click he makes when he comes in the door. *Where's my princess?* he says, and she runs to him and it is warm where he hugs her. In the winter, he smells of cold air, and she loves to press her face into his coat when he hugs her. She watches as he loosens his tie and changes into his other shirt. The hair on his chest is like that of an animal, strong and soft. She asked him once when she would grow hair like his, but he only laughed, and now she knows that only men have hair, and she is not a man. It would be good if she were a boy, because then he would not have to worry about her.

At dinner, he will tell her about his day. He works in an office with computers; he fixes the computers for the lawyers who work there, because they do not know how to fix them themselves. Her father says he is the boss. He says he tells them what to do all day long, Bill and Steve and Joanna. Sometimes, Bill gives him a hard time, and that is bad. Miranda wonders if it rains in the office when he does that. Joanna is old and slow, and Miranda hopes that when she is grown, her father will let her come and do the work Joanna does. She knows that women go to work and her father says yes, but she does not have to worry about that now.

He asks her about her day, and she tells him about the work that she has done. Almost always, he is pleased, because she has done it well. When he is pleased, he smiles and the room is warm and filled with light. When he is angry . . . he does not get angry at Miranda. Miranda is a good girl. Sometimes before bed they exercise together: sit-ups and jumping jacks and running in place. She can feel herself getting stronger every day.

On the table in his bedroom is a clock with no hands, where the numbers move and change themselves. Now she sits on his bed and watches the numbers change, five into six, six into seven, seven into eight. It is six forty-eight. Most days, he is home just before six. She closes her eyes, feeling fear in her mouth. Curling away from the clock, she puts her thumb in her mouth and rubs against it with her tongue. She will go to sleep, and when she wakes up, her father will be there. Sleep does not come, but she wills herself into another place, a place she goes to when she is frightened, where she rides on the back of a winged white horse and where the sun is warm. There is an island that she read of, where the water is blue and warm and outside it is safe. Her horse carries her over the island, and there are blue dolphins in the water far below. Words leave, and her mind is filled with pictures, and the feeling of a horse's muscles between her legs and the sun beating down. She watches the pictures in her mind and does not think. Then she opens her eyes and rolls toward the clock. Seven fifty-three. "Daddy?" she says, but the house is still.

Perhaps he is hiding, playing with her. Miranda walks through the silent apartment. She opens the closets and pushes back the clothes. "Daddy?" she says, but he is not there. She goes to the kitchen. Whimpering, she kneels on the floor, pressing her back against the cool of the refrigerator. He is not coming back, and she wonders why he has left her. There must be something she has done, and it is her job to figure it out so that he can come back. She twirls a piece of hair around her finger, and brings her thumb to her mouth to suck. "Daddy?" she whispers. "Daddy? Daddy? Daddy?"

The refrigerator hums against her back. She closes her eyes and sees him lying on the street with long, rubbery snakes twined around his arms. They are pinning him down, hissing and flicking their tongues in his face, and he is screaming, *Miranda! Miranda, help!* She sees him thrashing on the ground, twisting his head as they coil tighter and tighter around his wrist. . . .

He has not left her. He would not leave her. How many times has he promised: *I will never, never leave you.* But it is not his fault. They have gotten him. They are killing him, as they killed her mother (not-mother).

"No!" She must be strong. She is strong. She stands up and goes to the living room window. Outside, it is dark. People are walking back and forth under the streetlights, men and women carrying brown leather briefcases, hurrying with bent heads into doorways. Often, she sees her father coming down the street. Perhaps if she closes her eyes and counts to one hundred without looking, she will see him when she opens her eyes. She counts slowly, squeezing her lids together so that no one can say she peeked. It is terrible to close her eyes, to see the snakes sink their fangs into her father's face, to see the blood pour out of his cheeks, but she keeps her eyes closed and she counts. When she opens her eyes, he is not there.

And then she knows. It is a test. The Voice comes on

in her head as though someone has turned on a radio. It says, *Find him.*

"I can't," Miranda whispers. She hears laughter echoing within her skull. *You can't therefore you must therefore you will.* Frightened, she curls up on her bed, pulling the covers over her eyes and listening to the Voice. *You will you will you will.* The Voice scares her, and so she leaves her body and sits near the door, watching herself as she gets up from the bed and goes to the closet to look for shoes. She watches her hands pull past the folded sweaters and broken toys, sneers at herself as she roots like a pig after an ancient pair of Mary Janes. She had worn them on the last day of first grade, the last time she had gone outside, the day before her mother went out the door. As she touches the shiny black leather, Miranda comes back into herself. She holds one shoe against her nose and smells the world and rubs her teeth against her lip. Gingerly, she places the shoe against her foot. It is much too small. Perhaps it has shrunk, alone in the dark closet for all these years, as her mother warned her that she would shrink if she could not learn to say no. She pushes harder, trying to force her foot into the shoe, but it is impossible. The Voice mocks her. *Barefoot and pregnant, barefoot and pregnant, barefoot and pregnant.* Words her father uses. If she goes out in bare feet, she will be pregnant and her father will kill the baby and then he will kill her. She must wear her father's shoes.

In the hall closet is a pair of old sneakers that he sometimes wears outside on rainy nights when he goes to the store to get after-dinner treats. Her feet slip easily into them, and easily out again with each step. She begins to cry, and she hears her father's voice call louder and more insistently: *Miranda! I need you! Hurry! Hurry!* She sobs and leaves again as her body balls newspaper to stuff in the toes of the shoes. When her hand reaches up to open the lock, Miranda is far, far away.

And then she is on the street, and the air is cold against her face, pushing against her face like the air from the hair dryer in the bathroom, but this air is moist and stings where it touches her cheek. She moves her feet forward and there are bumps that pop up to trip her so that she stumbles, lurching forward, and then arms reach out to her and she pulls back and presses against the stone front of the building, panting as the people hurry by. There are smells in the air and noises that she does not understand, honking, barking, shouting, laughing, talking, swirling in her ears like dust, and the stones are rough against her back, unyielding as she presses up against them, but they will not help her find her father.

Daddy, she thinks, and then she forces her feet out into the street, and she is looking and not looking, because she needs to look to find her father but is afraid to look because the men on the street can kill her with their snakes, as they long ago killed her mother-not-mother. With her lids pressed down she can watch through her eyelash haze, the lashes like bars across her lids so that maybe she is in a cage and can be safe. There are people on the street, millions and millions of people that feel hard when she bumps against them, and voices shouting, "Hey, kid! Open your eyes! Look where you're going!"

There are colored lights that sparkle like jewels and tell her whether her father will be safe or will be dead, and she stands and watches them for a long, long time, trying to read what they say. She looks away and sees a man take a snake from a large metal box. He wraps it in blood and bread and gives it to another man. Miranda watches, not watching, and when the man begins to eat the snake she screams and runs, head down, into the street, past honking cars and voices yelling, "Crazy kid! You wanna get yourself killed?"

I can't find you, Daddy, she thinks. *I want to go home.* Her breath comes in sobs. *I want to go home. I want to go home.* And then she knows: there is no home. She left and her father told her not to leave and now he has made home go away and she is lost forever. She thinks of the warmth of her room and the soft-moving past days that are still and quiet and safe with folders and peanut butter sandwiches and her father tucking her into bed at night and the loss is too much to bear, but it is all, all gone. Her face is wet and she swallows her tears. Again she hears the Voice: *Find him.* She remembers that her father is lost, too, both of them lost in the swirling noises. If she can find her father, he can take her home. *I will, Daddy,* she thinks. *I will.*

Eyes squeezed almost shut, she moves like a bat, grazing solid shapes, then veering away. She feels cold, and knows because she has not been cold before that she is dying. The snake-man has killed her. It is all right, because her father is dead and her mother-not-mother is dead, and she will be dead, too. She smiles because that *was* the test. Her father is dead, and the place to find him is death. *You see, Daddy,* she thinks. *I will find you, after all.*

Her legs are cold and heavy beneath her. She is running and running into death, and then she feels the earth grow softer and the lights are gone. She is in the park. She reaches out and the tree bark feels rough and unyielding, like her father's skin. Wrapping her arms around the tree, she rubs her cheek against it until her face begins to hurt. Then she curls up at its feet and waits for death.

Chapter Two

Abby Cohen sighed. The community meeting was not going well. The ten ragged bodies before her were draped like cast-off clothes, uninhabited and inert, on hard plastic chairs arrayed in a circle. The only noise was the ticking of the clock. Her own body, almost six thin feet of it, shifted restlessly against the unyielding seat, and her teeth rubbed against her lower lip, scraping off the pale pink lipstick she had applied that morning. She tasted the soft clay flavor and felt vaguely ill. Although she told herself she would reapply it later, more likely she would not. She seldom glanced in the mirror, and when she did, her appearance generally failed to register. Since she had grown old enough to care, she had found herself unattractive. Plain, she might say. The kind of girl about whom it was said, *But she has beautiful eyes.* And indeed her eyes were beautiful, bottle green as glass washed up onshore from the sea. Not that it mattered, she thought. Better not to be too pretty in her line of work.

She looked from one kid to another, taking them in.

A few, dressed in jeans and T-shirts, might have been high school kids visiting the hospital for a term project. The rest in some invisible way were marked as damaged, the kind of kids you would not sit next to on the subway. Her eyes settled on Freddy, a tall seventeen-year-old veteran of the ward. His eyes obscured by long, dark bangs, he was pressing his body into his chair as though he could mold himself into it. Their eyes met briefly and he looked away, laughing softly to himself. *No.* She moved her gaze around the circle. Natalie, an obese girl with bulging eyes, gazed around the room unseeing, her mouth hanging open like a beached fish left too long in the sun.

Abby scolded herself. She was working too hard. It was not her job to run the meeting; she was there only to supervise. But the psychology interns whose job it should have been had just rotated onto the unit, and looked as scared as the teenagers they were to heal. The clock ticked again and she stifled another sigh. The silence was filled with boredom, as the air held old smoke and sweat, but there was fear, as well, the unbearable anxiety of sitting too long with thought and uncertainty. Beside her, Simon's leg began to jiggle. As if at a signal, Tim began to pick his nose with vigor, transferring the mucus into his mouth with a rapid shuttlelike motion. Like animals around a water hole, the children sensed an unseen danger and set themselves for flight, or fight.

"Claudia?" Abby said, addressing the intern closest to her. "Perhaps we should get started."

"Right." In faltering tones, Claudia introduced herself and then paused. Abby felt Freddy grow rigid beside her; he sensed the weakness. "How 'bout it?" Claudia started, wading into the silence. "Any issues? Anything come up that we need to discuss?"

Natalie spoke. Sixteen years old, five feet four, she weighed close to two hundred pounds. Her hair, matted and unwashed for weeks, hung down her back. "When can I get my clo-othes?" Her voice was a whine, high-pitched, grating. The nurses hated her. She was in her hospital pajamas because she continually tried to escape—elope, as the staff called it. On her last admission, four months ago, she had gotten out in her pajamas and walked all the way through Central Park in the snow before anyone stopped her.

Abby sighed. "That's not a community issue, Natalie. That's a personal issue. You'll have to talk to your doctor about that."

"Which one is my doctor?"

Her doctor was a new psychology intern, Claudia Weiss, a slim, pretty woman who had begun her rotation on the ward only a week before. Her face wore the same expression of stunned, repressed terror as many of the patients'. Looking at her, Abby was reminded of the first days of her own internship, when she had stepped onto a floor filled with acutely psychotic men and women and heard the doors lock shut behind her. It had been the best professional experience of her life. Perhaps it would be so for Claudia, as well. "I'm your doctor, Natalie," Claudia said in a friendly tone. "Remember, we spoke about this yesterday."

Natalie scanned her face and then looked away. "I want a different doctor. I want my old doctor."

"I know," Abby said. "It's hard to lose someone you

care about." In St. Ann's, a teaching hospital, interns and residents rotated on and off the unit every four months.

Freddy leaned forward in his chair, long legs jiggling, his acne-pocked face intense. "Well, I think Dr. Weiss . . . is nice," he said.

"Why, thank you, Freddy," said Claudia.

Freddy's smile became a leer. "I'd like to drink her up, on ice."

"Freddy!" Abby said.

"We could do it once . . . or do it twice."

Abby half stood. "Do you need to leave the meeting, or can you control yourself?"

"I want to crush her in my love vise."

"That's enough!" Abby said. "You need to leave."

"Run my fingers over her like mice."

Abby went to the door and called Bernard, one of the nurse's aides, a large black man whose muscles strained the sleeves of his T-shirt. "Freddy needs some help getting back to his room," she said.

Freddy stood, looping his thumbs through the belt loops closest to his crotch. "I'm going, I'm going," he said, and walked to the door. He was almost out when he turned to Claudia. "Anytime you want to fuck, I'm your man. Slice and dice, Dr. Weiss." His laughter echoed down the hall, harsh in the sudden silence of the dayroom.

"Well," said Abby, "any thoughts? Any reactions to what just happened?" Nothing. "This needs to be a safe place," she said. "We all need to keep this meeting safe." In the filtered gloom of dust-filled sunlight, no one spoke, and the room lapsed back into silence.

After the meeting, alone in her office, Abby sipped the cold coffee she had brought with her that morning and stared out the window into spring. Later, she would have to summon the empathy to comfort both Freddy and Claudia, but now she just felt annoyed. When Claudia's eyes scanned the group, her glance mingled pity, compassion, and fear in an amalgam that burned like acid on the ward's raw-skinned children. Freddy was no match for her, really; Abby had seen him curled in a fetal position on his bed, trembling, when she walked down the hall past his room. Too much caring was terrifying for these kids. The paranoid ones viewed it as a plot, while the rest, unable to feel deserving, either retreated in confusion, acted out against it, or seeped toward it like water to a sponge, seeking absorption.

Not that it was ever easy to find the right balance. When she remembered her own internship, it was with a red-hot embarrassment that made her cheeks flush, still, after all these years. She had been so scared at first, conjuring images in her mind. They were psychotic, the people who inhabited the locked ward she would share. Crazy. Raving lunatics. She had lain awake the night before she started, picturing filthy, shouting men pushing overflowing shopping carts down Broadway through the rancid heat of a summer day. There had been some of those—it was true. But there had also been Eleanor, a lithe and lovely former dancer whose first psychotic break had tripped her like a foot stuck in an aisle, a cruel practical joke. And David, a thin Jewish mystic whose delusions were almost poetic in their endless complexity. She smiled, remembering the pity she had felt, and the myriad ways they had found to use that against her.

So she had learned to keep her distance, offering warmth without intimacy, empathy without pity. It became easier with time. Michael had made it easier, and later her children, Sarah and Ben. Then she had not needed her patients to need her so much, to fill empty spaces in her life.

Abby put her cup down on the desk. The coffee was disgusting, with cold milk and melted wax congealing in ribbons on the surface. The seminar she was giving, Working with the Suicidal Adolescent, began in half an hour and she had not reviewed her notes since last year. It was time to get moving, but she could not bring herself to rise from her desk.

It had been happening more and more of late. She would be humming along, propelled like a self-winding watch by the rhythm of her routine. But as soon as the job was done, her sense of purpose dissipated, as well, and she was overcome by inertia. She was like the postencephalitic patients she had seen in a movie, who might freeze in the middle of brushing their hair and remain frozen until somebody came to move them. Like them, Abby, too, might sit for an hour on the couch, holding a cup of coffee, her mind not so much a blank as a river flowing randomly over stones as the warmth seeped out of the mug and into her fingers. It frightened her, this drifting off. When, with a superhuman force of will, she finally yanked herself up and back into action, she was aware each time of a deep sense of loss, and a longing to be back there in her mind instead of bruising against a world where nothing more than the grumpy "Excuse *me*" of a stranger in the subway could snap the thread of meaning and leave her weeping shamefully in the middle of a crowd.

The phone rang. "Hi, sweetie."

Michael. They had been married for ten years and known each other for almost twenty, and she still felt herself quicken at the unexpected sound of his voice. "Michael, hi."

"How's your day?"

"Oh, the usual." She told him about Freddy and Claudia, making an amusing anecdote out of the disaster. "And you?"

He was having trouble with a patient, he said. He wanted her advice. As he launched into his story, she felt her mind begin to wander. She heard the rumbling bass of his voice rather than its words. It didn't matter. It was not her advice he wanted, not really—just the quiet of her listening to give form to thoughts that it helped him to speak aloud. Often, she felt she could put him on hold and be just as effective.

"Right?" he asked.

"Mmmm-hmmmm." Sometimes she felt that they had known each other forever. They had been children, practically, college seniors, when they had met. Her roommate had been dating his, and mentioned to her one day that her boyfriend had a friend they thought she would like. Later, he had paid another guy ten bucks to replace him as her Secret Santa, the one assigned to do something nice for her at least once every day for the week before Christmas. She remembered: a lobster dinner; a squash lesson with the captain of the squash team; an afternoon when, silent and smelling of snow, he had entered her room and led her blindfolded to the shower, where he had washed her hair with firm fingers and apricot shampoo. It had been a week filled with magic, and on the last night she had come home from the movies to find a Christmas tree dressed in tinsel and lights, sparkling in the middle of the living room floor, with Michael sitting beneath it, smiling, wrapped in velvet ribbon, whispering, *Didn't you know it was me?*

He had seduced her before she knew it was he. But there were other things, too: the strong, square cut of his hands as he helped her frame and hang a picture in her room. The deep, quiet, almost feminine way he listened as she talked, and never interrupted to offer advice until she asked. The broad arc of his shoulders as he slammed a tennis ball across the court, playing singles for the intramural team. And the soft, warm press of his lips against hers, the lazy probing of his tongue. *Slow down,* he told her once. *I want to memorize you.*

She had not wanted to fall in love with him. She had been applying for a Marshall Fellowship, which would have paid for her to study in Vienna for a year. But when the time came, she found that he had seeped inside her like water, both buoying her and weighing her down. *I guess I don't want to go after all,* she said, and he replied, *Then don't.* And then she had let herself fall, and it was like the sweet release of fear that she had heard occurs before drowning.

After college, they moved to New York together, found a walk-up apartment, took out loans for graduate school, and ate spicy noodles from each other's chopsticks at their favorite restaurant on Amsterdam Avenue. And never, never had she regretted her choices, because in narrowing her life for him, she found it growing deeper than she had imagined it could grow. It wasn't his fault the bottom had fallen out.

His voice in her ear faltered and trailed off. "Are you listening?" he asked.

"Of course. And I think you did the right thing."

"Really?"

"Really." When had he begun to need this reassurance? she wondered. He had always been self-assured to the point of arrogance. They chatted briefly, working out the logistics of the day. He would pick up bread and milk at the store; she would get home early to relieve the sitter. "Oh, and ice cream," she reminded him. "I think we're running low."

"Done."

"See you home."

"See you then."

Then she was up. Clinging to the chain of mindless motions that pulled her through her day, she put down her coffee cup, scooped up her notes, straightened her skirt, and turned off the light. "If anyone calls, tell them I'll be in around four," she said to the secretary. And then she was out the door.

Chapter Three

"Oh, shit," the policeman said. "Another kid."

"Dead or high?"

"Who knows?" He poked her with his stick. "Hey, kid, you alive in there?" The body stirred, pulling tighter into itself. "Alive," he said.

"That's good, I guess."

"I guess." He poked her again. "Rise and shine."

Miranda opens her eyes and it is morning and she is not dead but sees a man with a snake about to bite her. She screams and tries to run, but the tree reaches out to trip her with its foot and she is falling, and the man is grabbing her arm and so she leaves and watches herself from far away.

"It's okay, kid," the policeman said. "No one's gonna hurt you. What's your name?"

Silence.

"Where do you live, huh?"

Silence.

The policeman looked at her face, squeezed tight in terror. "Bad trip, I guess."

"Shit, the stuff that's on the street now . . ."

The other man tried to make his voice sound gentle. "Can you tell us where you live, hon?"

Silence.

"Your call," he said to his partner. "Take her or leave her?"

The partner looked down at her. "She can't be more than twelve years old. We better take her."

"You got it. Come on, missy," he said, pulling the girl to her feet. "We'll take you somewhere you can come down safe."

Miranda is in Bedlam. The room is long and dark, lined with formless sheet-draped shapes that writhe and wail on cots along the walls. She sits beside the snake-men, awaiting death and wishing, wishing, it would come soon. The voice says *want something to eat,* but it is a strange voice and she does not understand what he means. The woman is in front of her with a white coat and moving mouth: *What is your name where do you live tell me did you take anything any drugs any crack any PCP any LSD can you hear me boy she's really out of it huh better take her upstairs let me just draw some blood.* Then the snake is coming closer, biting her arm, and she screams and flails and they hold her down and the snake bites her and draws out her blood with its fangs while another snake bites her bottom and the stinging venom seeps in.

When Miranda wakes up she is sad because she is not dead, and she wonders why the snake did not kill her. Her room is small and there is sun in the window, so she thinks perhaps her father is alive and knows she has tried to save him. Her cheek hurts her and her mouth is dry, but the juice in the refrigerator is far away or gone, and she has no one to buy her any more. She curls on her bed and counts her fingers, then traces around the sun shapes on the white sheets. It is quiet and she feels grateful for that. A woman comes in and says *Hi, I'm Dr. Weiss what's your name I'm here to help you can I ask you some questions what's your name can you hear me oh well okay I'll come back later why don't you get some sleep* and then she is gone.

Miranda lies on her bed and watches the sun shapes move across the sheet until they fall off the bed and spill onto the floor. When they are gone, a woman comes with food on a tray. She is not to waste food and so she eats it, soft white mashed potatoes and soft gray meat and soft green peas and soft red Jell-O, and the apple juice tastes like the juice in her refrigerator and so she smiles. It is good to lie still on the bed and not to think but just watch the shadows move in the hallway outside her door. The woman comes back and says *All done, good girl, come with me I'll show you where the bathroom is my name is Laurie and I'll be your nurse.* Laurie was the name of her mother-not-mother and Miranda feels frightened. She understands that they are telling her that they will kill her soon, as they killed her mother. This woman is taking her to death, but she goes, and it is not death but a toilet, where she can pee as she does at home, and then she knows that they are toying with her, waiting to gain her trust, and she laughs to herself because she knows they never will.

Laurie takes her back to her room and gives her two

pills and some more juice and Miranda takes them and waits for death.

Abby sat in her office, rushing through her notes so that she could leave in time to celebrate the first night of Passover at her parents' home on Central Park West. Haggadah reading began at six o'clock sharp. One did not come late. The clock on her desk read ten minutes before five. Her eyes paused, staring at the Sisyphean journey of the second hand sweeping past six and then struggling up again.

So many minutes. Sixty to the hour, almost fifteen hundred to the day. How many minutes in six years? Not enough. And so many wished away . . .

She remembered Sarah's infancy, time expanding like water to fill the aeons of each gray predawn gloom. Hours she had sat, heavy-lidded, exhausted, feeling tears spill down her face as her tiny Dracula slowly drained her of life. *Sleep, baby, sleep.* Anxiously waiting for her to sleep through the night, take the first step, say the first word, poop in the potty, grow up already. If only she had known.

Thinking about her daughter now felt like entering a garden, walled off from the rest of the world, where memories hung like overripe fruit, and the recollected slap of flip-flops against the hot pavement or the smell of sunscreen and ocean water could resurrect the entire brief life of a child. For on the day that Ben took his first step, Sarah had gotten sick. It started with a cold that would not go away, and bruises that appeared from nowhere. One year later, she was dead. Two years ago, Sarah had died. And those memories, too, hung heavy in the garden.

In the months after Sarah's death, she had been told repeatedly that time would help her heal, and to some extent she had found that true. In time, the searing pain that had consumed her had been battled back, so that instead of her being lost in it, the pain was inside her. If time were truly linear, she thought, it might have carried her away, leaving the pain behind. But it was not. Instead, it curved in on itself, like a serpent's coils, always ready to strike. Passover again, the third since Sarah's death, the third spring that brought rebirth to the forsythias and daffodils and lilacs in the park while passing over her daughter's corpse. Once, she had loved this holiday, with its familiar story and familiar food but without the greedy rush of presents that marked so many others. Not now.

She had just written the last of her patient notes when the phone rang. "Hi, Dr. Cohen. It's Claudia. I'm sorry to bother you so late, but I wanted you to take a look at this new kid they just brought up."

Abby sighed loudly. "Dan Naik is on in five minutes. Can't it wait for him? I'm really trying to get out of here."

After a pause, Claudia replied, "I guess. But she's not talking at all, and men seem to scare her. . . . Look, whatever you think. I just wanted to run it by you."

It never failed. Almost always, Friday's fragile, mute admit would be Monday's demand to be released right away. But in her mind, Abby always imagined the headline in the *Post*: DRUG VICTIM DEAD AS SUPERVISOR LEAVES EARLY ON FRIDAY AFTERNOON. Better to take a look. She called home to tell the babysitter to have Ben ready to go by five thirty, and went to rescue Claudia.

★   ★   ★

Miranda opens her eyes and sees shoes in the doorway. Her eyes move up and see that the woman is tall, but she does not look at the woman's face. The woman's voice says *Hi*. She comes slowly into the room and sits in a chair near Miranda's bed. The room is quiet. Miranda looks at the woman's necklace. A flower of delicate golden threads hangs between the woman's breasts. Miranda looks at the necklace and the woman sees her looking. "It belonged to my grandmother," the woman says, and she takes it off and holds it out to Miranda so that she can touch it. It feels cool between Miranda's fingers. She gives it to the woman, who puts it over her neck so that the flower hangs between her breasts once more. The room is quiet for a long time. The sun has gone from her window and the light is gray, so the woman's face looks blurred. Miranda looks in her eyes and they are the color of her father's tea. She thinks about sitting at the kitchen table with her father, wrapping her fingers around the warm mug when he let her have a sip. The woman is talking. "Can you tell me what happened?"

It is her father's request: *Tell me what happened today.* When Miranda answers, her voice sounds unused and strange in her ears. "My father is dead and they were killing him and then I went to find him but I was lost."

"Who was killing him?"

"I don't know."

"How did you know he was being killed?"

These are the wrong questions and the wrong answers. Miranda can feel her heart beat faster and stronger and she feels frightened. The woman is quiet again. She is sitting in a shadow and Miranda would like to be in a shadow, too. She does not know when the woman will leave, and does not know if she wants her to leave. Slowly she feels her heartbeat soften. The woman is looking not at her but out the window, and Miranda looks through the window, too, at the lights outside.

"I want to help you find your father," the woman says. "But I'll need to know your name."

My father is dead, Miranda hears inside her head, and then she understands that they must find his body so that he can lie safe in the ground and his soul will be still.

The woman's voice is soft in her ears, like a cat rubbing against her skin. "Can you tell me your name?"

Miranda whispers: "Miranda."

The woman smiles. "That's a beautiful name. Do you know your other name? Your last name?"

Miranda does not understand. Last name? There is only one.

The woman tries again. "Do you know your father's name?"

"Daddy," she says, surprised that the woman would not know.

"That's your name for him. What do other people call him?"

"I don't know."

"Okay," the woman says. "That's okay. How about your mother's name?"

Miranda feels her arms and legs go stiff and her breath comes in gasps. She has told too much. *Don't talk to strangers,* her father says. She rolls into a corner of the bed and listens to the rain. She has been bad, very bad. Her father is very disappointed in her. From far away she hears the woman's voice: *Where do you live what's your address what's your phone number what did I say what happened what happened okay you'll be okay you're safe here* and then the woman leaves and the room is quiet until they come with more food and more pills. Miranda eats and then lies still, waiting.

Chapter Four

Outside, the April dusk felt moist. Abby's admission note in Miranda's chart had been brief, just enough to cover her in case something did happen over the weekend. After meeting the girl, Abby judged her suicide risk to be fairly low. Miranda seemed too bewildered to muster the will to act with any purpose, but sometimes they could surprise you. Anyway, it was Claudia's problem now. She could make the phone calls, try to find the family. Abby had her own family to deal with, and as usual, she was running late.

She emerged from the clammy subway air into a deep blue dusk, and began walking west, toward Riverside Park. She had always loved this first view of the feathery trees, looking in their spring silhouette as though they had a three-day growth of beard. She watched Nick, the hot dog man, slather mustard and sauerkraut on a hot dog and hand it to a man in a blue jogging suit. Her mouth watered. When Sarah had been small and Michael still building his practice, Abby and Sarah had often eaten picnic suppers in the park. Together, they would pack a small cooler with all the things they loved, noodles smothered in Parmesan cheese, turkey, pickles, strawberries, and grapes, and walk down to the river, munching their food and watching the boats drift by.

Funny, now that Michael was home much earlier, there never seemed time to take Ben. Never time to do anything with him, it seemed, other than get him dressed, make sure he was fed. Oh, she did all the things with him a mother should do. She read to him and played with him and pushed him on the swing, but all the while she knew that she was only playing a part. She felt hollowed out, like a pumpkin scraped dry inside. Soon she would begin to rot.

She turned south on West End Avenue, acknowledging the nods of the doormen and weaving her way around children playing catch over awnings. Ben knew, too—that was the worst of it. She would catch him sometimes, staring at her, watching and waiting with a gaze too intense for his chubby face. And once, just before sleep, he had said it: *You're not my mommy. Where did my mommy go?* She had no answer to give.

Feeling herself begin to sweat, she slowed her pace, opening her coat to the river breeze. Winter had been easier, when she'd bundled herself against the cold. She did not want to slow down or breathe deeply. Life was stirring on the trees, in the ground, mocking her. Perhaps they should move to Alaska.

As she neared her building, she felt a familiar sense of dread. There would be the too-sweet smiles from some neighbors in the elevator, the carefully averted eyes of others. She felt like the Medusa of 680 West End Avenue: look at her and turn to stone. Today, though, she was in luck. Sam was on duty in the elevator. Hired only a few months ago, he was not yet elaborately kind. He let her off on her floor and she paused outside her door, unable to bear the click of her key in the lock.

At last she opened the door. "I'm home."

"Mommy! Mommy!" Benjamin, four years old, wriggled out from behind the couch and ran to her, trailing dust. Abby noticed with annoyance that he was not dressed. Another thing to discuss with the sitter. She had, after all, *specifically* called home with one simple request. She almost never asked for— But then Ben was jumping up against her legs, lifting his arms to her. She hoisted him up and swung him into the air. "Hi, sweetie. How's my boy?"

"And do you know what?" he said, as though they were continuing a conversation.

"I give up. What?"

"Me and Lolly went to the zoo and she let me get POTATO CHIPS and there were baby monkeys."

"Potato chips, huh? You're a lucky boy."

"I know. And guess what?"

"What?"

He giggled. "I can't tell you."

"Oh, come on. What?"

"You have to guess."

Abby eased him down onto the floor. Her watch said five forty-five and he was not even dressed. She could feel a pounding in her head as she walked away from him, toward the kitchen. "Honey, we don't have time. We have to get ready for the seder. We're already late."

"Guess!"

"Let's go find Lolly. Maybe she can help you get dressed."

"Mom! Guess, I said." His tone was imperious, just short of weepy. Great. All she needed at the seder was a cranky kid. God, it was hard to come home sometimes! She wished that there could be some few moments of transition, a freeze-frame where she could read the mail, have a glass of wine even, change her clothes, before the onslaught began. Fine, she would guess. "You saw the seals get fed."

"Nope, wrong!" he shouted triumphantly. "Guess again."

"Ben! I give up."

"One more guess."

And so it always was with him, one more, one more, one more, until suddenly she was yelling at him and he was shrinking into frightened tears. "One more. One. Let's see. . . . You saw the polar bear playing with his toys."

"Wrong! One more guess."

Abby let out her breath in an exasperated sigh. "Ben, no. I said that was it. Now tell me or don't."

He looked at her out of the corner of his eye. "Okay. But I have to whisper. It's a secret."

Abby knelt down and he moved her hair with his sticky hand. His breath was warm against her ear. "One of the monkeys had a red bottom. And he was *pooping!*"

"No!"

"Uh-huh."

"That must have been pretty funny, monkey." She scooped him up, cradling his legs against her hip. "Now let's go find Lolly."

"She went home already," Ben said, speaking as though to an imbecile.

"She went home? Well, who's taking care of you?"

"*Daddy,* silly. But he's in the bathroom, so now I'm taking care of myself."

That explained it. Michael had undoubtedly come home early to help out, and then, letting Lolly go early, forgot about the helping part. Had Lolly stayed, Abby could have come home to a ready-to-go boy, but now . . . She marched into her bedroom and plopped him down on her bed, where he bounced his legs up and down like a bronco as she changed. "Yi-haw!" he yelled. "Ride 'em, cowboy! I'm a horse, Mom," he added helpfully.

She ignored him as she changed into a clean blouse, brushed her hair, and put on fresh lipstick. "Now it's your turn, kiddo. Let's get you dressed, too." She pulled off his dirty shirt and pants, tossing them into her hamper. He trailed her into his room and watched her getting clothes from his drawer.

"I want to wear my sweatpants." He sat on his bed in his Superman underwear, with his back against the wall and his arms crossed over his chest. Cloth balloons, red, orange, green, yellow, and blue, flew above his head against the white wall.

Abby held the pants across her legs. "Well, you can't wear your sweatpants tonight. This is a party, with Grandma and Grandpa and Aunt Kate and Uncle Josh and Jonathan and Mandy. Everyone is going to be wearing real pants, and you need to, too."

Ben stuck out his lip and shook his head no.

"Why not?"

No answer. Just the same stubborn tossing of the head, back and forth. "I'm going to count to ten," Abby said. "And if these pants aren't on by the count of ten, there will be no computer time tomorrow. Ready? One . . ."

Ben sat.

"Two . . . three . . ."

"I hate the computer. It's boring."

There is probably a better way of handling this, Abby thought, but it was too late to back down now. "Okay, then. Just remember that tomorrow. Four . . . five . . . six . . ."

"But why do I have to wear those pants? I hate those pants."

Ah, an opening. Abby sensed capitulation. "You can choose another pair if you want. Just not sweatpants."

"Well, I hate *all* my pants except my sweatpants."

"Seven . . ."

"They're baby pants!"

"Eight . . ."

"Hi, Daddy!"

Michael stood in the doorway, tying his tie. His straight brown hair, still wet from the shower, was slicked back from his forehead. Every angle, every edge, of his face was familiar as he stood there: the jutting arc of his nose, the brown eyes flecked golden and green like leaves swirling in a shallow stream, the rough, stubbled padding of his cheeks. When she thought of him during the day, she had trouble putting the face together. Working down his face in her mind she could conjure each feature, but she could never make them gel, so that seeing him, each evening, she was filled with the shock of the familiar. And each time, she thought, *Ah yes, so this is who you are.*

Tonight, he looked fresh scrubbed and smelled of soap. "Hi, honey," he said. "I had a cancellation this afternoon, so I stopped by the gym on the way home." He kissed her cheek. "Make up for your mom's matzo ball soup tonight."

"How nice for you," she said. *Thanks for getting everything ready around here.* She didn't say the words, but he must have heard them in her tone, because he turned immediately to Ben.

"Are you giving your mother a hard time?"

"Nine," Abby said, motioning for Michael to go away.

"No."

"Looks like you are."

"Nine and a half."

"Mommy wants me to wear these stupid-head pants and I don't want to."

"What do you want to wear?"

"Ten!" Abby said. "Michael, please. We've been through this. He wants to wear his sweatpants and I said no. Now put on your pants, Benjamin. This instant."

"Daddy!"

"Why do you want to wear the sweatpants?" Michael asked. "You'll look silly at the party, when everyone else is all dressed up."

"Because I like them. I hate those other pants. They're poopy pants."

"Why are they poopy pants?"

Abby glared at Michael. "You're not helping." To her, he seemed a caricature of a bad analyst as a two-year-old child, always asking why when what really needed to be done was to get the pants on and get the hell out of there. He would stand there and reason with Ben until they had it all worked out, even if it took hours. And Ben, she was sure, would make it take hours. She could scream! Who cared why he thought they were "poopy pants," anyway? Tomorrow he might love them. Michael did not seem to understand how arbitrary Ben's world was. He didn't have reasons for half the things he did—any more than she did, probably. She spent her whole day searching for hidden meanings, deeper reasons for crazy behavior. At home, she just wanted to get moving.

She sighed, suddenly seeing the other side. Maybe she should just let him wear his sweatpants. Michael would. Why did it really matter what pants he wore? What did matter, though, was that she was the bad guy, as usual. And they were late. And she was close to tears.

"I'm just trying to see if there's a compromise here," Michael said.

"Well, there isn't. I've told Ben to put on his pants. Now either tell him to put them on or please go away and let me handle it." Mean mommy. Mean wife. At least she was consistent.

Michael turned to Ben. "Do what your mother says."

"Dad-dy." Ben looked betrayed.

"Now."

The game was over. "O-kay." He stuck out his short, solid legs and allowed Abby to slide them into the pants. "But I'm not wearing shoes"—he smiled coyly at Michael—"unless Daddy helps me put them on."

"Fine," Abby said. "You want Daddy to help you—then Daddy will help you." She threw down the shoes.

Michael looked exasperated. "Would you rather do it?"

"No, thanks. You go right ahead."

"At least it'll get him dressed."

"Right. Yes. Thank you very much." Abby left the room, hating them both. Ben and Daddy, Daddy and Ben. The apple juice she poured wasn't as good as Daddy's apple juice. She didn't know how to read the story the right way, the way *Daddy* read it. For Daddy, Ben would put on his pants, put on his shoes, button his coat, wear a hat, hold hands across the street, do whatever needed to be done. With her, everything was a battle. Even at night, in the middle of a bad dream, it was Daddy he cried for, Daddy he wanted. Never did he seem to want her.

But where was Michael when *she* woke in the night? The endless patience he had with Ben evaporated when she turned to him and tried to talk. And the longing for him she sometimes felt curdled at his touch to rage and bitter nostalgia. So she lay next to him in the dark, trying not to think or feel, letting herself be conscious only of the solid warmth of him just beyond her skin. But then he was stroking her breast, nuzzling her ear, pawing, needing, taking, wanting to make love, and turning away in sullen silence when she said no. Never, anymore, did he ask *her* why. And she learned not to lie on his shoulder, not to touch him at all, until their bed became cleaved in two, as though they had hung a sheet across the middle for modesty, like Clark Gable did in *It Happened One Night*.

He had loved Sarah, too, of course; his loss was as huge and unthinkable as hers. Still, he never mentioned Sarah's name voluntarily, and refused to have any pictures of her on public display, where his eyes might fall on them when he was unprepared. In the weeks after she died, while Abby lay doped up and stupid in bed, he had gathered all the pictures together and put them in a box, along with a few of her dolls, her green flowered overalls, her artwork, and her stories. Abby had never seen him look in the box, but she did sometimes notice pieces of yellowing paper on the quilt near his pillow. Once, maybe a year ago, she had asked him if he wanted to go through the things with her. He had shaken his head and left the room, and she never asked again. She often felt him wish that he could put her into a box, as well, just another painful reminder of his little girl.

His refusal to share Sarah's memory struck her as strange, since Michael was by nature a hoarder. His key ring bulged with keys to apartments he had long since given up, to bathrooms in offices he hadn't worked at in years, to summerhouses long since leased to others. She remembered when they had begun dating, how jealous she had been when an old girlfriend would call to chat; she hadn't realized that Michael gave himself to others so fully that he was bound to keep them in his life, if only to keep himself whole. And now the piece that he had given to Sarah seemed gone for good.

It all stemmed from his childhood, he had explained. But you didn't need to be Freud to see that having a father, as Michael had, who drove off one day to buy groceries and never returned would turn anyone into an emotional octopus, wrapping his tentacles as tightly as possible around all of those he loved.

Don't leave me, he had said to her in the midst of their falling in love. *Don't ever leave.* And she had promised him then that she never would. Just once, before marriage, before children, when the ticking of his clock in the silence of her bedroom pressed against her ear like an alien heartbeat and threatened to drive her mad, she had gone off to Europe alone. She had bummed her way across France and Italy until at last she reached Greece. On a beach in Corfu, alone and unafraid, she had stripped off her bathing suit and waded naked into the warm water. The water was calm and perfectly clear, and as she looked below the surface at her own naked breasts and thrashing legs, she felt, for the first time, beautiful.

When she had come home at last, she had found Michael waiting, patient as Penelope, to welcome her back and she had chosen to bind her life to his. It had been a good life, after all. Sometimes she thought if she had only gone for good, only married someone else, had a different child, then Sarah would never have been born and would never have died. She had given him her trust and he had taken her into the wrong life. This had never been supposed to happen, not to her. She could never forgive him for that. Perhaps it was only anger after all, but as she stood in her room, listening to the voices of her husband and son outside her door, she wished herself back on that beach, swimming alone through schools of fish as her strong arms pulled her through the water and her hair streamed out behind, like a mermaid, free.

They appeared in the doorway, Ben looking handsome in his gray pants and brown shoes. He was her son, after all, her little boy. She remembered him as a baby, grabbing her hair, stroking her cheek, clinging to her when she left the room. *My little ball and chain.*

"You look great," she said, smiling.

Ben stuck out his tongue. "Well, you don't!"

"Benjamin! That's not a nice thing to say!"

He shrugged and ran down the hall as Abby stood, listening to his footsteps.

"Come back here!" she yelled. "That was really obnoxious, you know?" But he was gone.

Well, fine, she thought. *I don't love you, either.* And there it was, a stone dropped into the still well of her mind, sinking as the ripples spread: unnatural, frigid, rejecting, bad, mad, much too sad. *I'm sorry,* she thought. *Oh, God, Ben, I'm sorry. Go to Daddy. Be with Dad.*

"Come on, Ab! Elevator's here!"

"Just a second." She looked at her image in the mirror, ran her fingers through her hair, and tried to smile.

"Mommy! Come *on!*"

Of course you love him, she told herself, and hastily brushing powder onto her cheeks, she went to join her family.

It was hard for Abby to go from the dark of the taxi to the light and noise of her parents' apartment, festively flowered for the holiday.

"They live the closest, so they come the latest," Abby's father, Aaron, said at the door as he helped Ben get his jacket off.

"Sorry," Abby said, feeling the sting of her father's constant criticism. "Someone had a hard time getting dressed."

"Now, Michael," Aaron joked, "I thought you'd outgrown that stage."

Michael looked contrite. "I didn't want to wear my pants."

"Daddy didn't want to wear pants and neither did I!" Ben shouted, running into the living room. His grandmother, Ruth, caught him in a hug. Behind her, Abby could see her sister, Kate, and Kate's husband, Josh, getting up from the couch, looking crisp and calm as they nibbled on carrot sticks and waved from their wrists, like royalty. Abby felt a familiar stab of pain at the sight of her niece, Amanda, who sat close to her mother's side, her sleek brown hair tied back with a velvet ribbon. She was eight years old. Sarah would never be eight.

She willed herself to smile. "You look so pretty, Mandy. So grown-up."

"Thank you," Mandy said stiffly. And then she opened her arms to Ben, who raced over for a hug. "Didn't want to wear pants, huh?" she said. "That's silly."

"It certainly is," Ruth said. "Because otherwise your legs might have frozen right off, and then we'd have had to carry you everywhere."

Ben looked up from his cousin's embrace. "That's silly."

"Better watch who you're calling silly, young man," Aaron said. "Your grandma cooked the food, so you'd better be nice if you want to eat."

Ruth motioned toward the dining room, where the table was covered with a white linen cloth, and the crystal wine goblets twinkled warm in the light from the candles. "Speaking of eating . . . now that everyone's finally here why don't we start so the natives don't get too restless before dinner is served?"

"I'm sorry we were late—" Abby began.

"No, no, not at all. But it's Ben who's going to get hungry, you know."

"Yes, Mom. I know. I said I'm sorry."

"What's for dinner, Grandma? Is it pasta?" Ben asked hopefully.

"Even better than pasta." Ruth led him to his chair and helped him into his seat. "Matzo ball soup, gefilte fish, brisket . . ."

"Eeuuu, gross! I hate that!" Ben stuck out his lip. "I want pasta."

Ruth gave Abby a look. To Ben, she said, "Well, matzo ball soup is like pasta. You'll like it—you'll see."

"No, I won't," said Ben. "I hate it."

"That's enough!" Abby said, sliding into the chair next to his. "Eat it or don't. We don't care." She turned to her mother. "He's been impossible all day."

"I want to sit next to Daddy."

"You will, you will—don't panic." Abby got up from the chair and gestured to Michael. "Will you please sit next to your son, and ask him to cut out the nonsense?"

"Cut out the nonsense, son," Michael said, his voice mock-serious.

Ben giggled. "Nonsense, nonsense, nonsense."

"Non-fence," said Amanda. "Non-pence."

"Non-hence," said Mandy's brother, Jonathan, who

had just turned eleven. "Non-whence. Non-dense, non-mense, non-clense."

"Non-heckledejeckledepeckledeJENCE!" shouted Ben. Abby looked around the table at the laughing faces and suddenly she remembered a night on Martha's Vineyard, when she was eleven years old. They had been at their summer home, a beachfront cottage, and she was angry at her mother, who had taken her sister's side in an argument, as she always did. Abby had been told to leave the dinner table and she had gone for a long walk on the beach, crying, skipping stones into the water. She remembered standing on the dark beach, shivering slightly in her T-shirt, and looking up through the large glass window of their house, where Kate sat laughing at the table with their mother in the warm yellow kitchen, both held in a circle of light from the lamp above their heads. Abby knew that all she had to do was walk up the beach and through the door to be welcomed into the circle again, but at the same time she felt that the light was not big enough to hold all three, and that it was somehow right and proper that she be the one left out, alone, on the dunes.

If they really loved her, she had thought, they could have tried harder to break down the wall she had erected and become trapped behind. But they never did. It was with her still, as her father began reading from the Haggadah. She was alone in the room, a one-woman diaspora in the family tribe. She watched as Ben poured salt on his plate and smoothed it into patterns with his finger, remembered doing the same thing as a child. She could feel the rough grains of salt as they rubbed against her skin, the delicious sting on her tongue as she licked them off. How strange to be the grown-up, when her remembered feelings from long ago seemed more real to her than the emotions she was experiencing now. Across the table, Jonathan whispered something in Mandy's ear, and Mandy told him to quit it. Aaron looked at Jon. "Then Moses said, 'Let my people go.' And Pharaoh said—"

"No!" the children shouted. Ben looked up and smiled. It was his favorite word.

"So God sent plagues upon the people of Egypt," her father went on, telling the story he had told every year of her life. "And there were—"

"Blood!" they all shouted, flicking drops of red wine onto their plates. Ben laughed, loving the grown-ups' spills.

"Frogs!" Another drop of wine.

"Lice!"

And Aaron's sonorous voice intoned, "But Pharaoh still said—"

"NO!" Now Ben was shouting, too, caught up in the story.

"So God sent more plagues. Wild animals!"

A drop of wine.

"Sickness!"

Another drop.

"Blisters! Hail! Locusts! Darkness! And Moses said again, 'You see my God is a mighty God. Will you let my people go?' But Pharaoh still said—"

"NO!"

Aaron's voice got softer, pulling everyone toward him as he spoke. "So God sent the worst plague of all, the killing of the oldest child. But first he told the Jews, 'Take a lamb bone and make a mark above your door. I shall tell the Angel of Death to pass over all houses that bear that mark. The rest I shall mark with death, even if that house be Pharaoh's house.' And he killed the oldest child in each Egyptian family, and killed Pharaoh's oldest son, as well, and when Moses asked again, 'Will you let my people go?' Pharaoh finally said yes."

As Abby listened to the story, she remembered the night that Sarah had died, when she had come home and glanced at her daughter's unmade bed. *No tears,* she told herself now. *Later, you can cry.* The faces around the table were glowing with candlelight and wine; Ben was bouncing in his chair. She picked up her cup and drank. Amen.

Finally, the Egyptians were drowned, and the afikomen was duly hidden. "All right now, gang," her father said. "Let's eat."

Chapter Five

The days are strung together like stitches in the woman's knitting, each neatly cast off, bound and finished, before the next begins. Symmetrical and safe. Miranda sits in the dayroom and watches the woman's needles, which are like long silver nails protruding from her fingers, but not scary because they do the woman's bidding, over and under, over and under, making a soft, warm sweater out of the red wool. The needles are an animal with quickly moving glinting teeth that devour the yarn and spit it up again, transformed. Hour after hour the woman knits and Miranda watches. She is not allowed to stay in her room during the day, so she sits in a brown chair and listens to the waves of noise from the television on the wall and the voices of the others, strange sounds that do not seem like words, as though they speak a language that she does not know. She eats and takes pills, white and orange, goes to the bathroom, stands under the warm shower, and rubs herself with liquid soap that is no more to her than that. One day the short woman shows her pictures of bloody butterflies and

women's private parts being ripp[e]
swords. When Miranda is done a
what she thinks, she knows to say
But she needs to warn them: *Be careful*
These pictures can kill.

The nurse is named Laurie. She tel[l]
have not found her father because Mir
phone and is not able to tell them her a .... voice
sounds harsh and Miranda knows that she means her father
is dead. The voice that came from the air has gone quiet. No
one tells her to find her father, and that, too, must mean that
he is dead. Perhaps she did not have a father. Perhaps she has
always been in this place of rough white sheets, soft food,
and stitched-together days. Perhaps there is nothing to feel
sad about, after all.

She does not feel sad. Instead, she feels the soft
weight of the hospital robe against her skin, the sharp stabs
of pain when her teeth bore into her tongue, the dull
metal taste of blood inside her mouth. She tries hard not
to wonder why.

Sooner or later they will kill her, too. All the eating,
the long, slack hours in the dayroom . . . her father has told
her about fattening pigs for the kill. She is a pig. The pills
may be poison or the food may be poison or the water may
be poison. She does not know, nor does she refuse anything
that she is offered. She is in their hands, to do with what
they will. Already her mouth feels dry. It is difficult for her
to speak, and she must ask for water often. Her body is stiff,
too, as though they are turning her into a machine. Many
days, she wants only to sleep, but she will not allow her eyes

re the others in the dayroom, and they will not
ne in her own room until dinner is done.

Miranda looks up. The tall woman is standing in the
doorway, and she smiles when she sees Miranda's face. She
beckons for Miranda to follow her, and she does. They go
into the woman's office, which has shadows on the wall that
flicker on and off as the clouds blow by outside her window.

The tall woman tells her that she will be her doctor
and Miranda thinks again that she is not sick but will be sick
and then the doctor will not cure her. "How are you feeling?" she asks. It is a trap.

Miranda sits, silent. She has told this woman too much
already, and the woman has done nothing except let them
kill her much too slowly. She has not found her father; she
has not taken her home.

"Okay," the woman says. Even sitting, she is very tall,
long and thin, like a snake. Miranda thinks, *Perhaps she knows
who killed my father.* She smiles and the woman sees her
smile. "Something funny?"

Miranda shakes her head no, and the room is still. Miranda watches the shadows on the wall, and wonders if the
woman can tell her what they mean. The woman follows
Miranda's eyes. "Shadows," she says, and Miranda knows that
she will never reveal their secret. "Pretty, aren't they?"

Miranda nods her head yes, and the room is still. The
silence feels good around Miranda's ears. She likes the way
it holds her in the chair. It is hard to fight the noise all the
time, to be rattled and jarred with thoughts put into her
head and taken out again against her will. She has never
been used to noise. The quiet feels good and lasts a long

time. "Thank you," she says. The woman looks at her with a question in her eyes, but Miranda is still.

In the afternoon, on her way to the elevator, Abby looked into the dayroom. Miranda was sitting exactly where Abby had left her hours earlier. Her eyes, with their shoots of color, like fragments of glass from a broken mirror, were half closed, and her blank, dead face was hidden behind her hair. Abby felt that if she were to take Miranda's hand at that moment, it would crumble into dust. She seemed oblivious to the noisy arguments in the room. Her eyes were empty.

As Abby watched, Miranda took a piece of her hair and twirled it around her finger, exactly as Sarah used to do, and Abby was struck with a sudden, terrible longing to circle her with her arms and hold her as she had held her daughter. She turned away so that Miranda would not see her tears. *It's all right,* she wanted to whisper. *It's going to be okay.* But she did not know to whom she was speaking: Miranda, Sarah, or herself. And it had not been okay. Sarah had died, and with her died Abby's innocent faith in the inevitability of happy endings. She was not specially blessed, after all.

Of course, Abby knew better than to say any of these things to the faded girl who sat before her now. Instead she said nothing except good night, but Miranda, shrunk into herself, did not even look up.

Miranda lies on her island in the warm sunshine. Her horse has carried her there. There are no snakes and the sand is soft under her body. There are peaches to eat, swollen with juice that runs hot down her chin, where she licks at it, cat-like, with her tongue. She is a cat, stealthy, independent, un-afraid, purring in the warmth and sweet stickiness. There are children on the island, brown and small, who join hands with her and pull her up. They form a circle and begin to dance, around and around, faster and faster, and Miranda laughs as the dizziness overwhelms her and she finally falls with the others back onto the sand. She lies with them, laughing. And then the wind turns cool. The children are gone, and she is alone. It is getting dark; soon it will be night. She begins to feel afraid. She wants to bury herself in the sand, but the warmth has gone and it feels rough against her skin. She rolls onto her stomach so that she cannot see and listens to the wind blowing around her ears and the buzzing of the flies, and waits.

"Our girl seems to be settling in," Miranda's nurse, Laurie, told Abby at the staff meeting a few days later. "I saw Na-talie trying to teach her checkers this morning, and they were playing some kind of game this afternoon."

"Natalie! You're kidding! Not the one I would have picked for her."

"Like Mutt and Jeff. But you never know. I thought I saw her smiling, but of course I couldn't be sure, behind all that hair."

"Is she talking more?"

Claudia Weiss rolled her eyes. "Not in group. All I get is a sphinx stare and a Mona Lisa smile. But never at me. Kind of at a spot on the wall, above my shoulder."

Laurie nodded. "Not to me, either. But sometimes they need to talk to each other first."

"True."

Bill Dolman, the unit's psychiatrist and titular boss, had been listening quietly and doodling on a yellow pad. "Maybe it's time to up her meds."

Abby scribbled a note. "And we'd better get social work involved in finding this father, don't you think? If he is dead, we're going to have a hell of a time with a discharge plan. And if he's not—"

"If he's not," said Claudia, "why the hell hasn't he called? You'd think he'd be frantic."

"Yup," Abby said. "You would, indeed." It occurred to her that maybe he *was* dead, this mystery man, Miranda's father. "You know, we may be dealing with some posttraumatic stress here. If her father *were* murdered, and if she even saw it, maybe . . ." Abby paused.

Bill shifted in his chair. "Just a reminder," he said, without looking up. "We have absolutely no insurance information on this kid. She's already been here, what, two weeks? We're eating all the costs. Everything. Now I don't want to be the bad guy here, but we're not a foundling home. Either we find this dad, soon, or—"

"Or what?" Abby said. "Or we boot her out on the street?"

"Calm down," Bill said. He put down his pen and looked at Abby for the first time. "I'm not Simon Legree. But these kinds of cases go to the state. We need to start calling around, Kings County, Bronx Psychiatric, see who has a bed in Peds."

Abby felt her face go hot. "Absolutely not." Her voice was louder than she'd meant it to be.

Bill raised an eyebrow, then looked down and resumed his drawing. "Can we remain professional here?" he asked, his voice calm, condescending.

"I don't know," Abby said. "Can we remain human?"

Bill leaned back in his chair and crossed his arms across his chest. "I resent that," he said. "I'm sorry that money has to come into these decisions, but that's just reality and you know it. Do you want to pay her bill? What is it now? Seventeen days at one thousand a day, plus meds, plus therapy, plus testing, comes to—"

"Fine." Abby wished, suddenly, that she could just take Miranda home herself. She could have Sarah's room.

The rest of the staff had been silent during the exchange, but now one of the social workers spoke. "I'll call Tom Connally," she said, referring to the hospital's lawyer. "Maybe he can figure something out."

"Good idea," Abby said. "Why don't I make the call?"

"When do we cut bait?" Laurie asked. "Tell her that maybe her dad *is* dead?"

"I don't think it matters what we tell her, actually," Abby replied with a sigh. "I don't think she hears a word we say."

Miranda likes the girl with the dead beaver on her back. She asks where the girl got the beaver and the girl laughs and says *First you have to be black, honey, and then you just don't let them wash your hair for a long, long time. You get a beaver, all right, and no one touches it. Stinks, though, don't it?* Miranda smiles because she likes the smell of the girl: pungent, like the hamper in the bathroom, where the wet towels live. She likes the game they are playing, too, where the checkers can move only on the black squares, because the red squares are blood and the board is a river of blood but the black squares are safe. And if you are jumped, you are killed but not really dead, because you can come back as a king. They play over and over, until Miranda wins a game and Natalie knocks the checkers to the floor and says *Bitch*. Then Miranda picks up the checkers and plays the game by herself.

Time passes. Hours and days. There are no lessons and no books and no clocks with flipping numbers, just a line on a dial that struggles from bottom to top only to fall again. She has no idea how long she has been here, how long her father has been dead. Now she stands in line behind Natalie, waiting for her turn to get the orange and white pills and the small paper cup of apple juice. They watch her as she swallows, and look inside her mouth to see that the pills are gone and maybe also to look at her tongue. She thinks that perhaps the medicine is for her tongue, to loosen it up in her mouth or make it bigger, so it will choke her. Her tongue feels larger to her, and her mouth is dry. There will be more juice with breakfast. She goes into the dayroom and sets the table as she has been shown: forks on the left, knives on the right. The forks and knives are made of dull white plastic and Natalie says it is because if the knives were real they would all kill themselves. The eggs are yellow and slippery. Yesterday, they fell onto Miranda's lap when she tried to take a bite, and a girl with a spotted face laughed at her.

She eats and the food slides down past her swollen tongue. Natalie says *Hey, Miranda, you'd rather watch cartoons than news, right?* and Miranda nods. Natalie turns toward Freddy and says *See* and Freddy says *She's a fucking catatonic anyway and her vote doesn't count.* Natalie turns toward Freddy again but looks past him and Miranda follows her gaze to the door, where the tall woman is standing. Miranda feels herself smile and then quickly wills her face flat.

The tall woman comes into the room and stands next to her. "Good morning, Miranda. Are you almost done?"

Miranda nods. The food is there and she eats it and then it is gone. It fills her inside like a baby, pushing her stomach out against her underwear. She is getting bigger every day; she can see it in the shower when she rubs the soap against the swellings on her belly and her thighs. Her father had not liked it, these swellings that erupted, softening the straight lines of her body. He frowned when he looked at them. Disgust. They disgusted her, too. *You're growing up,* he said, accusing her, and bought her loose clothes to hide her shameful parts. *You should have been a boy. I would not have to worry then.* She closes her eyes, feeling her shame. Her father has left her.

When she looks up at the tall woman again, she sees her hair as fire over her head, which burns but does not consume. Her father has told her about such flames, and also the flames of hell, where bad girls go, but Miranda is a good girl and will not go to hell where fire can burn beyond recognition . . . and then she smiles. She knows! She wants to leap in the air with glee, but she keeps herself very still, because of course it must be a secret. "Mommy," she whispers, very low, and, looking up at Abby once more, allows herself to smile.

Actually, Abby was glad for an excuse to call Tom. He was young, only a few years out of law school, and . . . *unscathed* was the word that came to mind, with an easy confidence and a ready smile. Where she saw ambiguities and layers of questions, he saw only answers. Plus, he was easy on the eyes, as her friend Melanie always said. He had a young man's lean body, a boyish face with eyes of a blue so pure they looked like a child's crayoned drawing, and curly dark hair whose fringes brushed the base of his collar. She felt herself blushing as she punched his extension into the phone.

He answered on the first ring. "Tom Connally."

"Yes, by God, it is," Abby said. "How did you know?" She picked up a pen and began to doodle on the pad in front of her, staccato lines crisscrossing into webs across the page.

"Abby?"

"Two for two. You're on a roll."

He paused, and she could almost see his smile. "What's up?"

She shifted the phone to her other ear and leaned back in her chair. Talking to him, she was reminded of conversations she used to have with her boyfriend in high school, long, rambling discussions that served to maintain a connection rather than exchange information. "Remember Miranda? The new patient I was telling you about?"

"I think so, yeah. The mystery kid, right? No family, no visible means of support?"

"Right."

"I remember. How's she doing?"

"Really well, actually. And that's the problem."

"Naturally."

"Because—"

"Let me guess. Bill."

"He thinks she's ready to move on."

"And you don't." It was a statement.

"And I don't. Neither does he, or at least he wouldn't if he thought about it. But you know—he's under a lot of pressure."

"Trim ship and all that. Believe me, I know."

In the pause that followed, Abby realized that the designs she was sketching with her pen had grown softer, the lines now traveling in waves and curls, forming shapes that could almost be hearts. One of her friends in graduate school had proposed that they do a joint dissertation on the psychological implications of doodles. Embarrassed again, she scribbled over her creations, then tore off the page and tossed it into the trash.

"So how can I help?" Tom asked.

Take me to a desert island, she thought. *Spray me with whipped cream and then lick it off.* She found herself stifling giggles, struggling to compose herself. "I just want to get a sense of what we can do. Are there grants we can use? Get the state to pick up some of the cost? Can we get her committed? What are our options here?"

"Hey, that reminds me," he said, changing the subject. "Did you ever see that skit—it was *Saturday Night Live,* I think. That bank that only made change for people." He made his voice go down a register. " 'Give us a ten—we can give you two fives, or a five and five ones, or even ten ones.' Remember? And then, like, 'It's all about options.' "

Abby laughed. "Right. And then he said, 'People ask me all the time, how do you guys make money? And I tell them, *volume.*' I love that one." She paused. "But seriously, about Miranda. What are our options?"

"Yours? You have none."

"Tom."

"I'll check, all right? Off the cuff, it sounds like you have three. No, four. Either get her on a grant somehow, find her father, or lie low, and hope Bill forgets about her."

"And the fourth?"

"Take her home yourself."

"Thanks. I already thought of that one, actually."

"Why doesn't that surprise me?"

Abby lingered, unwilling to hang up. "Anything new with you?" she asked lamely.

"Nothing much. I've got a meeting, actually, so I've gotta run. Keep me posted, though, okay?"

"Sure." After he hung up, she held the phone to her ear for some time, unwilling to break the connection between them, the dial tone humming in her ear. She felt vaguely disoriented, as though she'd just returned from a distant voyage and was suffering from jet lag. She was not sure where she'd been, only that it had felt warm and nice, and that she wanted to return.

Chapter Six

The string of days grew longer, and suddenly the mid-day sun was hot, shining through the windows of the dayroom and lighting up swaths of tiny dust motes that danced around the frozen children who sat there. Gradually, beneath the light, some of the patients began to thaw. Natalie stopped talking about killing herself, and even allowed her hair to be sheared. Without it, she seemed lighter, freer, even happier. Freddy would be leaving soon, to stay with an aunt and uncle until his mother got out of jail. Even Miranda seemed to be awakening. No progress had been made in finding her father, and Abby, having gotten some bad news about grants from Tom, had chosen to go with option three, lying low. So far, Bill had not mentioned Miranda again, but she knew it was only a matter of time before he did. Meanwhile, the girl was beginning to trust. Her eye contact was better, and she was talking more, and more co-herently, in their sessions.

Abby had begun to take Miranda outside for their talks. There was a patio on the eighth floor, enclosed with steel-mesh walls, where patients were sometimes taken to play balloon volleyball or just get some air. Abby would sit on a chair while Miranda gingerly approached the edge, looking down in wonder at the streets below as though they were new to her.

In their last session, Abby had looked at Miranda's spindly legs, loosely wrapped in her hospital pajamas, and wondered who could have cared for her and allowed her to drift into sickness without even an attempt at a cure. As she let her own thoughts wander, Miranda stood in silence in the sunshine with her hands splayed out before her, watching the light play on the tiny hairs of her arms. Her voice startled Abby, making her jump a little in her chair. "At home, there are no snakes," she said. "And the sun lives in Daddy's room."

"Really? All day, or only part of the day?" Abby asked.

"In the afternoon. In the morning, it wakes me up in my room, but then it goes away for lunch, and in the afternoon it is in Daddy's room."

"Maybe you're surprised that the sun can live in the hospital, too."

Miranda smiled, and Abby knew she was right. "I was surprised," admitted Miranda. "But you live here, so the sun can live here, too. Even without Daddy, I guess."

"But the sun is here even when I'm not."

Miranda was silent, but in the set of her shoulders Abby saw that she had heard and was choosing to ignore. There was a hint of anger in the way Miranda turned away, and Abby was curious to see how it would manifest itself. "What else can you tell me about home?" Abby asked, expecting no answer. To her surprise, Miranda rewarded her with a flood of information. Anger, it seemed, opened her up a bit. It was a useful thing to know, as were the details that Miranda suddenly divulged. Home, the girl said, was where Daddy left in the morning and came back each night to see her, where there was food and warmth and safety and the sameness of day after day of nothing but time unfolding as the sun moved from one room to the next. Home was where Daddy made water run hot and cold from the tap, where he made light when Miranda flicked a switch, where he brought food that she liked to eat, where he made the sun go up and down for her as though it were a yo-yo on a string, where night was a blanket that he threw over the blue sky, leaving holes for her to see the light so that she would not be afraid in the dark. Home, as Abby saw, was where Daddy was God, controlling time and space and comfort, a magician on a desert island, playing sleight-of-hand tricks to an audience of one.

"Was there ever a mother there, too?" Abby asked.

Miranda sees it is a test. Her mother, this mother, is asking about the other mother, the not-mother. She must not lie to her mother: it is wrong, and besides, her mother already knows. She is trying to see whether Miranda is a truthful girl. She thinks carefully about what to say, and then she answers, "There was a woman. Not a mother. She was bad and then she left, and Daddy was happy. And I was happy, too."

"Do you remember about before she left?" Abby asked. "Did you used to go outside?"

It seemed to Abby that the sun faded from Miranda's

face and that she could see the darkness behind her eyes. "No," she said, and her voice was small and tight. "I don't remember." She would not say any more.

That night, Abby had a dream. She saw herself walking naked through a barren arctic land, where the wind howled like wolves in her ears. Looking down, she could see her feet encased in clear blocks of ice. They were so heavy in the dream that she could barely lift them, but she knew that she had to keep moving. She was searching for something in the snow, and while she did not know what she was seeking, the sense of its importance was overwhelming. Her eyes hurt from the glare, but when she cried out in pain she found that her voice, too, was frozen. She felt overpowered by fatigue. Her feet were simply too heavy to lift anymore, and the ice was creeping slowly up her legs, coating her skin like glass. Telling herself she would rest only for a moment, she prepared to lie down in a snowdrift. She was about to close her eyes when she saw a man approaching in the distance, his face obscured by a fur-lined parka so that only his eyes, sky blue and piercing, were visible. At the sight of him, she felt a warmth suffuse her body, and as he lay down beside her she knew at once that she was going to live, and she sank gratefully into sleep.

She woke to a wetness between her legs and a sense that she was melting. She let her hand travel up her belly, to caress her own breast beneath her nightgown. Her nipple responded by growing erect, sending messages of pleasure to her brain. It had been a long time since she had let her body speak to her this way. For so long her breasts had suckled children, not men. When she had been home with Sarah and then baby Ben her body was climbed on and tugged at and snuggled against until her flesh became as sensitive as sunburned skin, chafing at a touch. She knew Michael had worried, sometimes, that in her hours home alone she might be hosting other men, but honestly, the thought had never crossed her mind. She had never even had fantasies of an affair. A week alone on the beach, yes, but never a second's worth of sex. And after Sarah's death, it was as though her flesh had gone numb, as impervious to touch as a corpse. Yet suddenly her body was awake, calling to her, conjuring visions not of her husband but of a different man, a slim, dark figure with blue eyes and a sardonic smile.

But it was Michael who greeted her in the kitchen when she finally arose. He looked up from his cooking when she entered, his face flushed from the heat.

"Good morning, merry sunshine. How did you sleep?"

"Pretty well, I'd say." She yawned and ran her fingers through her tangled hair. "And you?"

"Just fine."

"We're having French toast!" Ben said, smiling up at her from his perch atop the dishwasher.

"Mmm," Abby said. "My favorite."

"My favorite, too!"

"Really? I hadn't heard."

"Uh-huh," Ben yelled. "Uh-huh, uh-huh, uh-huh." Abby ruffled his hair, wishing he had come with a volume control. Her head hurt.

She poured herself a cup of coffee and wrapped her

hands around the warmth of the mug. "So what do you want to do today?" she asked.

"I don't know. Whatever." Michael carried the skillet to the table, transferring pieces of French toast onto each plate. Without thinking, Abby picked up a knife and began to cut up Ben's food.

"NO!" he yelled.

Abby stopped, the knife and fork suspended over his plate. "What?"

"Mommy!" He was whining now, close to tears. "You *know* I like to cut it myself."

"Oops. Sorry, sweetie." She switched his plate for hers. "Look, you can have this one. You can cut it all by yourself, okay? And I'll eat the other one."

Ben nodded, wiping his nose on his sleeve.

"How about the playground?" Michael asked. "Ben? Want to go to the playground?"

"Yeah!" He bounced in his seat and then turned toward his father. "I need some maple syrup," he said.

Abby reached for the bottle. "Please?"

"I want Daddy to do it."

"Ben, enough."

Ben looked at Michael, who carefully averted his gaze. "Please," Ben said, pouting. Abby poured some syrup on her own plate, and then paused before helping Ben, remembering to ask whether he wanted it on the top or the side. "Both," he said, struggling with the knife. "Unnnngh," he whined, frustrated. "I can't do it."

"Can I help?" Abby asked.

"No. Daddy."

"Michael?"

"Fine."

She watched as Michael rose to stand behind his son, covering Ben's hands with his own as together they sliced the knife through the soggy bread. Her food felt flaccid in her mouth. She took a sip of coffee to wash it down and pushed her plate away. The surge of life she'd felt in her dream began to ebb, and the day seemed to stretch before her like a desert, flat and bleak.

Beside her, Ben had finally begun to eat. "Know what?" he asked, his lips sticky with syrup.

"What?" Michael asked.

Ben giggled. "This is so gross." He began to laugh harder, crumbs of food tumbling out of his mouth.

Smiling, Abby said, "If it's that gross, maybe it should wait for later."

"No," Ben said, "I want to tell you." He swallowed his mouthful of food. "Lolly told me that I have *bugs* in my mouth."

"That's silly," Michael said.

"No, really, Dad." Ben was nodding vigorously. "It's true. Lolly said we need them because they're what tastes our food for us so we know if we like it or not. And that's why they're called taste bugs. You and Mom have them, too, Lolly said. Isn't that gross?"

Abby looked at her son's chubby face, lit with the pride of teaching his parents something new. He was looking at them expectantly, waiting for their glee or disgust that might mirror his own. Stiffly, Abby moved the muscles of her face into a smile, wondering why it felt so hard to give her son what he so clearly needed, a simple thank-you for his gift. She remembered a time, long ago, when Ben was not yet two. He had gotten a balloon as a favor from some birthday party he'd gone to, and had refused to let Abby tie it around his wrist, insisting that he could hold it. And when, inevitably, it had gotten loose and risen quickly into the sky, he had looked at her beseechingly and said, *Get it, Mommy, get it,* in a voice that was filled with an absolute faith. Now his eyes were questioning, unsure. And instead of laughing, she felt herself irresistibly open her mouth and say, "Not bugs, honey. Taste *buds,*" while Ben's smile faded from his face.

That night, in the dark, still foggy with sleep, she heard a little voice say, "Daddy?" Michael did not stir. Pulling herself awake, she opened her eyes and beckoned Ben to her side. "What is it, honey?"

"I had a bad dream."

She reached up and lifted him onto the bed, snuggling him under the covers next to her. "Tell me."

"I was a baby kangaroo," he said, his voice catching on tears. "And there was this bad guy who wanted to kill me, so I jumped into my mommy kangaroo's pouch—remember? Like we saw in the zoo? But there was already a baby in there and the mommy one said I had to get out and the bad guy was going to shoot me."

She felt sick. "That's awful, honey. And then what happened?"

"Nothing. I waked up." He looked at her, searching her face, asking without words a question to which she had no answer to give.

She felt the tears in her own eyes spill over her lashes, alighting on Ben's silken hair as she held him close. *I'm sorry,* she thought again, sorry for Michael, sorry for Ben, sorry for herself and for the family that, lacking its center, spun relentlessly into entropy. Her body felt weighted by sorrow, her arms almost too heavy to lift, yet somehow she scooped Ben up, held him close, and carried him back to bed, hoping that the pressure of her arms around him would convey a love that she could pantomime rather than feel. Then she sat with him in his cozy room, rocking him slowly as she listened to the city noises on the streets outside, until he relaxed his grip and settled softly into sleep.

Chapter Seven

Jack Reynolds was pacing the floor. Ten steps to the end of the kitchen, ten steps back. He gnawed on his knuckle, rubbing his tongue against the thick black hair that grew there. The sink, usually empty and scrubbed, was piled with dirty dishes. A half-eaten pizza lay curled and congealed on the counter. And Jack paced.

It had been weeks since he had gotten stuck on the number three train for two goddamned hours on his way home from work and had burst through the door frightened and apologetic only to find his daughter missing. It had been weeks, awful, terrible weeks of days curved inward on themselves like black holes, days of frantic calls to hospitals and morgues, asking if anyone had his daughter and hearing only *no*. Other than his daily trips to the pay phone outside, he had rarely left his apartment. He called in sick to work, telling his boss that he hoped the computers could take care of themselves for a while because he had a family emergency. He had lived on delivered groceries and meals, and spent his days waiting, missing her, longing for her, fearing her for the power she had somehow discovered, the power to destroy him. Like her mother, she had vanished. Walked out the door, walked out on him, betrayed his love and his trust and his care. Almost thirteen years old, a budding rose, she would be easy prey for the perverts and filth on the streets. He had told her that; she knew it; she had learned the lessons he gave her, yet out she went. Well, then, she deserved what she got. He had warned her. She would come back sooner or later, crying for her father, saying, *Yes, Daddy, yes, you were right about the world outside.* He wondered what he would do when she did come back. He could see her at the door: matted hair, scratched face, tearstained, pitiful, whimpering, *Daddy, Daddy, please . . .* In his mind he went to her, held her, and rocked her in his arms and said, *Shhh, shhhh, I told you what the world is like,* and smiled when she said, *Yes, Daddy, you were right—I will never, never leave.* Or he went to her and pushed her roughly out again and only when she cried embraced her tenderly.

He remembered her as an infant, born ten weeks premature, her tiny body plugged into so many tubes that there was no room left to stroke her. She had been so small that when he stretched his hand out next to her, her entire body fit between his thumb and pinky. If he had been allowed, he could have held her easily in one hand, but the nurses had refused to let him hold her at all, for fear he might dislodge a connection to the machines that were keeping her alive. So he had stood by her isolette for hours, watching her breathe, longing to hold her close. He had never wanted anything so much as he wanted to feel the softness of her skin next to his, and he had vowed, right then and there, that if he could only get his hands on her, he would never let go. How, he wondered, could she have done this to him? Her. Miranda. His princess, his pet.

For so long, even after she had gotten out of the hospital, she had been terribly small and weak. He remembered watching anxiously with Laurie as Miranda struggled to suck from a bottle no bigger than a doll's; they'd measured her intake in milliliters and her growth to the fraction of an ounce. For years, her face had looked so thin that her skin seemed translucent. He remembered sleepless nights spent doing nothing but watching her breathe, willing her tiny chest to expand and contract as though only his vigilance could maintain her. And now she could be anywhere, hurt and alone, with no one to protect her.

When she still did not come home, Jack's anger turned to fear. What if she was dead? What if she had only worried when he was kept out so late, stuck on that subway on the day that she had left? What if she had gone out only for an hour, to look for him, perhaps? She could be lost or hurt or trying to get home to him, his sweet little girl, who loved him above all else, who loved only him because he was all she had to love. She would never leave of her own will. He knew that. It was madness to think otherwise. He cursed himself for concealing their address, for refusing to have a phone. If she was lost, she would not know how to find him. He should call the police. And say what? That a twelve-year-old was lost? That she might have wandered away from home and not been able to find her way back? At best they would find her, and then take her away from him for good. He was not stupid. He knew that people would misinterpret his attempts to keep her safe, would read with their filthy minds something dirty or disturbed about a father trying his best to keep a beautiful daughter safe from the dangerous world outside. Children were taken away all the time. And so he stuck to calling hospitals, and then he paced.

Waiting. It's not like he hadn't had plenty of practice at that, after all. His whole childhood had been waiting, it seemed. There had been nights, even weeks, of dread-filled waiting for his father to sober up from a bender and come home, so that his mother would stop crying and get out of bed to make him something to eat. And worse, when his father was sober and home, was the waiting for him to start drinking yet again. There were the hours and days and years of waiting for the end of math class, with teachers too stupid to even understand his questions, or the end of English, where classes full of assholes made fun of him because the letters scrambled themselves before his eyes and they were too shortsighted to see that, fluent or not, his ideas, his insights, were light-years ahead of theirs. He had waited. He had waited for the days to end so that he could escape his tormentors. He had waited for the school years to end so that he could get away from the shitheads at school, and for summers to end so that he could get out of the house and away from his angry father and his mother lying loose and limp and soft in her bed. He had waited to grow up, get a job, get a family of his own.

And then he'd met Laurie, and it had felt like his waiting was done.

And then Laurie had gone, and he had vowed never, ever to wait for anyone again.

And now his daughter was making a liar out of him. And there was nothing to do but pace.

And finally she won. He could stand it no longer. He felt the madness, dancing around his ears with laughter and strange, jeering faces. She would destroy him. She had been so weak, but now she was stronger than he. Perhaps that was not so bad. But she would not escape so easily. He would track her down. Every day he thought of more places to call. Digging the phone book out of the closet, he wrote lists of all the runaway shelters and halfway houses and hospitals in the city. And each time he left, he taped a note on the door:

WELCOME HOME.

I WILL BE BACK SOON.

WAIT FOR ME HERE.

And then he went out and dropped a quarter into the pay phone and dialed.

He had never known that there were so many places to be sick in the city. He could picture them, though. He remembered when Miranda was born: filthy coughing bloody bodies in the emergency room with dirty screaming children running everywhere past him and his lumbering wife as they tried and failed to get someone's attention until the contractions came so fast and hard that Laurie collapsed screaming on the floor. As always, the squeaky wheel got the grease, but Miranda was a quiet child. She could lie unseen for hours, hurt, bleeding. She could die in one of those places before anyone found her. He dialed the numbers and said to each harried voice, *I believe you have a patient named Miranda Reynolds. Could you connect me to her, please?* Weeks and weeks of *nos*, of *I'm sorrys*, of *I'll check and call you back*. She was not in Bellevue, not at St. Vincent's, not at Roosevelt or St. Luke's or Beth Israel. Or they said she was not there. Perhaps they did not know. He had read of patients lost for weeks in the system as frantic relatives called and called, believing the worst, as anyone would. There had been lawsuits, he knew. Lots of money paid out for emotional distress. He kept calling. Not at Presbyterian, not at Mount Sinai, not at New York Hospital. She was making a fool of him. She was not in the hospital at all. She was far, far away, eating spaghetti and sucking the long strands into her ripe red mouth with a boy who was sitting across from her, laughing in a restaurant booth, licking sauce from her lips with his probing tongue. She was talking about her father, saying he was crazy, saying he used to keep her locked up when that wasn't true. She could unlock the door anytime she wanted to. She was always free to go outside. She knew that. He had never tried to keep her against her will, never. She stayed because she loved him, and believed in him to keep her safe. She would never leave of her own free will. He knew that. And then one day he called St. Ann's again.

The first thing they told him was that they had no record of a patient named Miranda Reynolds. The next thing they told him was that they did have a girl named Miranda, with no last name. Approximately twelve years old. And when he said, "Yes, yes, that's her, my daughter," they told him he could see her in the morning.

Jack felt his knees go loose. He grabbed on to the top of the telephone booth to keep from falling, resting his forehead on the cool silver metal. Behind him, a voice said, "Hey, buddy, almost done?" and Jack flipped him the finger without looking up. They had Miranda; that was the important thing. They had her, and she was safe. Tears stung his eyes and he blinked them back until lights flickered behind his lids. He would see her tomorrow. But why tomorrow? Why did he have to wait?

They were keeping something from him. She was deformed in some way, burned, scarred, half dead, with tubes up her nose. Why couldn't he see her that night? It was only ten thirty. Miranda never slept before eleven—he knew that. They watched the ten o'clock news together every night! Maybe this place wasn't a hospital at all. Maybe it was some kind of research institute where they collected lost, frightened children and injected them with horrible diseases to see if they could cure them. There was no point asking how she was. They would only lie to him anyway. He would need to see for himself. "Of course, I'd rather see her tonight," he said, trying to stay calm.

"I understand." The woman's voice on the phone was soft and soothing. "But really, it would be best to let her sleep. You can come in first thing tomorrow, if you want. Anytime after ten."

Cars drove past in the darkness, rushing by him like wind. "Planning on finishing up sometime this year?" the voice behind him said, but Jack did not even hear. In his mind, he was back at the hospital, watching the tiny hand of his infant daughter clutch the air as she fought against her restraints. *I want to hold her,* he had begged. *Please let me hold her.* And he had been told, *No. Later. Wait. Not yet.* Just as they were telling him now. He felt an impotent rage rise in him like gall, and he dreamed of screaming to this soft-voiced sentry that he didn't give a fuck what she said—he'd be there in fifteen minutes, like it or not. How he hated these little bureaucrats, who wore their tiny shreds of power like badges on their chests. They were pitiful, pathetic—that's what they were. But they had Miranda, and possession was nine-tenths of the law. So for now, he would play along. That was the way to go. Show them how docile you were, how easily led, until they let their guard down. Then you could get away with murder. "All right," he said, "ten o'clock. I'll be there."

Chapter Eight

The tall woman is speaking, her hair burning in the light. "Why don't we go to my office? There's something I need to discuss with you."

Miranda wipes her mouth with her napkin and puts her tray on the cart, as she has been told. In the office, the woman twirls a ring on her finger and seems afraid and then Miranda feels afraid. The woman takes a breath and Miranda takes a breath and the woman sighs and says *Your father is not dead* and the room explodes in light and Miranda's thumb is in her mouth and she rubs her tongue against it. "I talked to him this morning," the woman says. "He wants to come and see you."

Miranda looks at the woman and sees a tall, thin snake whose head is a ball of fire, and then the snake is gone and the woman is sitting in her chair and looking at her. Miranda understands that the woman has brought her father to life in flames and smoke, that she has gone to the valley of the shadow of death and brought her father up into the world. She understands that the woman is a god and she laughs with a sound that is almost a scream.

"Are you okay?" the woman says, and Miranda nods her head yes. "It's up to you," the woman says. Miranda laughs again; it is funny, because she is sitting with a god and she is still in her body and still in the room, filled with the food she ate, tasting the eggs on the back of her tongue. There is no fire in the room and she is safe and the god is good. The woman is talking: "You don't have to see him if you don't want to. It's your choice. It's up to you." Miranda nods. "Do you want to see him?"

Miranda does not understand what the woman is asking. The woman says that her father is alive and she can see him or not see him, but the word *want* is strange to her. Her father is alive and he will come to see her. Her father is alive! The words spill down from her mind and fill her mouth. "My father is alive."

"He is," the woman says. "I talked to him this morning."

"He is coming to see me," Miranda says, and her voice is filled with joy. If her father is still alive, then she, Miranda, must be good and the sun will shine and she will be safe.

Abby looked at the girl sitting across from her. Her face seemed suddenly luminous. "Can you tell me about your father?" she asked Miranda. "Does he take care of you?"

There was a pause, as though her words had to travel a long way to reach the girl. "He keeps me safe," Miranda said at last.

"He keeps you safe from what?"

Miranda blinked. "You know."

"I don't."

"The world is a dangerous place."

Abby looked around the room, at the framed Monet posters on the wall, her collection of seashells, shelves full of worn, multihued books. She smiled at the room's familiarity. And yet, she remembered bringing Sarah to her office one day when she was sick, when she had shaken her little bald head at computer and crayons, and finally rested on the purple velvet pillow on the very couch where Miranda now sat and cried because her skin was raw and everything hurt. "It can be, yes," Abby responded. They were talking about Miranda. "And how does your father protect you?"

"He keeps the snakes away."

"Snakes?"

Miranda was quiet.

"Are there snakes where you live?"

Miranda does not trust this god. If she can call her father from the dead, then she must know about the snakes. It is a test, but Miranda does not know how she is meant to answer. She will show the god that she is not stupid. Then her father will come and take her home and she will be away from the god and they will both be safe. "There are snakes outside," Miranda says. "You know."

"And your father keeps them away?"

"He does not make me go outside." There. She has said enough. Perhaps now the god will understand that her father has power, too.

"He doesn't make you go outside alone?"

"He does not make me go outside."

"So you only go when you want to?"

Miranda frowns. That word again. Perhaps the woman is lying to her. Perhaps her father is still dead; perhaps he is not coming. "When will my father be here?" Miranda asks, as though the question is a shroud that holds his body within.

"You want to see him?"

"When will he be here?"

Abby sighed. She wished that she could make Miranda see that she had a choice. *I can keep you safe,* she thought, *if you'll just let me.* But Miranda was looking at her with unblinking eyes, waiting for an answer. "He should be here soon. Visiting hours start at ten. That's, let's see"—she checked her watch—"about half an hour from now." On Miranda's face, Abby saw nothing. No flicker of joy or fear. "Do you want to take a shower before he comes?"

Miranda understands: the woman can smell her, the she-smell her father has warned her about. Her father likes it when she smells like soap. She nods her head yes, and the tall woman leads her to the shorter one, who will take her to the water and make her clean.

Abby rushed to her office and called Tom, glad again for the excuse to hear his voice. Miranda's reaction had surprised and frightened her. She had seemed happy, at first, to hear that her father had been found, but then she had simply gone dead, like a candle flickering out. Whoever he was, he seemed to have enormous power over his daughter. Whoever he was, he was going to want to take her home.

"Tom?" she said to his hello. "Abby."

"Well, hi there. I've been meaning to call you."

"Oh yeah?"

"Yeah. I wanted to find out what had happened with that patient you were telling me about."

Abby wrapped the cord around her finger. "We must be on the same wavelength, because that's what I'm calling about. You'll never guess who's risen from the dead."

"How many guesses do I get?" he asked, his voice low and gravelly in her ear.

"None. It's Miranda's father. Jack Reynolds is his name. I got a message this morning from Laurie. He called last night and demanded to see her. Of course Laurie told him that he needed to wait till tomorrow, which is now today, if you follow. Apparently he got a bit abusive."

"Really?"

"I don't know the details. He'll be here in about twenty minutes, and I need to know what our options are, in case he decides to make trouble."

Tom laughed. "Ah, the options lady. Tell me, what do you imagine he'll do? Are we talking broken kneecaps here?"

Abby ran her finger along the edge of the phone. The cord had gotten tangled again. "I was thinking more along the lines of wanting her out now, AMA."

It would be no problem, Tom assured her, at least in

the short term. The law was on their side. They could get thirty days without even trying, and probably more after that. He was sure. And that was why she had called, after all.

She kept him on the phone a long time, joking that she hoped he wasn't billing by the minute, but reluctant to give up the easy flow of his voice in her ear. "Listen, I've got a meeting in five minutes. I really need to run," he said at last. "But I'm free for lunch next Tuesday if you want to grab a bite?"

Abby looked at her calendar. She usually had lunch with the interns on Tuesday, but talking to Tom had made her feel defiant. They'd probably be happy if she blew them off. It would give them a chance to gripe about her. "That sounds great."

"Twelve thirty at Polson's. All right?" he asked.

God, it was easy. Making plans with Michael always felt like negotiating at Yalta, with every contingency, every feeling, every need, accounted for. This felt more like . . . fun. Fine, she said. She would see him there. She hung up the phone and sat for several minutes, staring out the window at the sunny day outside, before getting to her feet to go meet Miranda's dad.

Jack Reynolds stepped off the elevator into a long corridor that smelled to him of disinfectant, coffee, and buttery eggs. Dirty young girls and boys, already teenagers, shuffled up and down the hall in mismatched clothes and too-short robes, eyeing each other as they walked past with sultry leers, pouting with full, moist lips. None of them seemed sick. If they were sick, why weren't they in bed? Surely this was the wrong floor. They would not keep Miranda here; she would never survive. He straightened his tie and ran his hand through his hair. He was Miranda's father: neat, responsible, in charge.

He walked to the nurses' station and asked for Miranda Reynolds, who was expecting him. The nurse looked up sharply and scurried to do as he asked, which pleased him. He waited, watching, and suddenly he saw her! It felt to him as though his flesh turned liquid in that instant, his essence flowing toward her as she moved down the hallway. He had thought she had gone forever, like his mother, his wife, but Miranda had returned. Yet she looked different from how she had when he saw her last, rounder. Her face was ashen behind the wet, dark ribbons of her hair. She held her robe closed in front of her and he was glad. "Miranda!" he yelled, and she looked up and ran to him.

"Daddy! Daddy!" He caught her in his arms and held her close, rocking her gently back and forth. He felt her bones, whole, intact, and the soft flesh of her breasts as they pressed into him. He pushed her away from him and looked into her face.

"Are you all right?"

She nodded and tried to press against him again, but he held her by the shoulders and made his voice stern. "Do you see what happens when you leave?"

Miranda's eyes filled with tears. "I'm sorry, Daddy. But I wanted to find you. You weren't there and weren't there and I thought you were lost. The Voice said to find you. And then I got lost and they took me here."

It was as he had thought. He held her close again and

stroked her hair, smelling the shampoo scent. "It's all right. It's all right. Daddy's going to take you home."

Miranda nodded and pushed the hair back from her face.

"Now where's your doctor?" Jack asked. "Let's see what papers we need to sign to get you out of here."

Miranda pointed to a tall woman who wore a long green sweater over a paisley skirt. A woman? Miranda had a *woman* doctor? That was fantastic! It would be easier for him to get what he wanted out of a woman doctor. Men might give him a hard time, but he knew women, knew how to charm them. He thought of his own mother, soft, sweet, stupid—a cow who had cleaved to him like a salt lick until he couldn't stand it anymore and left home to join the service. He remembered the tears and snot on her puffy red face like pus oozing from a wound. *Sorry, Ma, I'm outta here,* because he couldn't stand seeing her sunken in her bed, staring unseeing at Technicolor lives spooling past on TV while he waited hungry and bored outside her door. She had driven his father to drink, and then driven him away, too— no one could stand it, the way she behaved all the time, like you weren't even there! And then she had up and died on him while he was overseas, and he had never seen her again. Served her right, was his opinion.

The woman was walking toward them. "Mr. Reynolds?" she said as she approached. "I'm Abby Cohen, Miranda's doctor."

A Jew! But then, of course, they all were. "Jack Reynolds," he said, holding out his hand.

Abby shook his hand and smiled. "I see you two found

each other." Miranda shied away from Abby, pressing herself against her father and shielding her eyes, as though afraid to look at her.

Mr. Reynolds spoke. "Thanks for taking care of Miranda. I've been through hell these past few weeks, I tell you. Now what do I need to do to get her out of this place?"

Well, thought Abby, *let's get right to the point, shall we?* She gestured toward her office. "Let's sit down and talk a bit first, all right? I think we need to decide what's best for Miranda. I'm not sure she's ready to leave just yet."

There they go again, Jack thought. Once they got their hands on you, they never wanted to let go. Always looking to squeeze out those last few insurance dollars. Well, they could find somebody else to con. His daughter was going home. "You're the doctor, of course, but she looks fine to me. No bruises, no broken bones. In fact, none of these kids look sick."

Abby looked at him. "Perhaps it would be best to discuss this in my office."

"I don't see why. Just give me the papers to sign and I'll sign them." He laughed bitterly. "Don't worry. I'll take full responsibility. We won't sue. I promise."

"That's not my concern."

"Well, what, then? She looks fine. A little fat, maybe, but we'll soon fix that up at home."

The other patients, sensing excitement, began to crowd around them. Natalie put her hands on her hips and grinned. "Whooooeeee! That your dad, Miri? He cute! Can I say hi? That okay? He cuter than my dad—that's for sure."

Freddy sidled up behind Miranda. "So he ain't dead after all."

Jack glared at him. "Apparently not."

Freddy thrust his middle finger toward Jack, then edged it toward Miranda's ass, wiggling it inches from her bottom and licking his lips. Abby stepped between them. "Aren't you supposed to be in class?" she asked Freddy.

"Yeah . . . but this is more fun."

She turned to Jack. "This would be easier in my office."

Jack nodded, and they turned together, leading Miranda with them down the hall and depositing her in her room before continuing to the office. Abby closed the door and motioned to the leather couch. Jack sat awkwardly, at the very edge of the seat, as though any minute he might rise to go. His stare was fixed on her face. "You're right," she began, trying to skirt his evident hostility. "Miranda's not physically sick."

"Go on."

"But she does have a mental illness." Abby ignored Jack's snort. "She has an illness in her brain that makes it difficult for her to think clearly. It makes her afraid when there's nothing to fear—causes her a great deal of pain, I think."

Jack snorted again and got to his feet. "Of course she's afraid. Who wouldn't be, in a place like this?" He walked to the window and looked out, keeping his back to Abby.

"You don't see any fear at home? No confusion? No strange behavior?"

"Of course not," he said, without turning around. "What would she be afraid of at home?"

The sunlight poured through the window, hurting Abby's eyes as she looked up at Jack. His bulk made a shadow against the glass and she tried to focus on his back, where the ill-fitting suit that he wore strained to cover him. "At school, then?" she said after a pause. "Have the teachers noticed anything unusual?"

Jack sensed a trap. Children who did not go to school were taken away. He knew that; he was not stupid. "No," he said, without turning around. "No one's said anything to me."

"Well, would you mind if I spoke to her teachers? It would help me to help her."

Jack turned around and stared at Abby, his eyes locked on hers. The sun shone directly into her face, and she shifted her gaze away. "I don't mean to be rude, but she won't be needing your help anymore. Thank you for taking good care of her. Now she's going home with me."

Abby stood and opened the door, scanning the ward for Bernard, the nurse's aide. He was flirting with the cleaning woman at the end of the hall. She took a deep breath. "I'm afraid that won't be possible. We need to keep her here at least a few more days, for observation. Of course, you'll be free to visit anytime, now that we know where you are."

Jack pictured that ugly, pimple-faced boy with the hand that wanted to grope his baby. He was right. This was no hospital. "Are you saying you will not allow me to take my own daughter home?" His voice was loud and angry.

"That you're going to hold her here against her will and mine?"

"Just for a few more days," Abby said weakly, "for observation."

"Bullshit!" Jack shouted. "You can't do that. This isn't jail. You can't just keep her here. I have friends who are lawyers. I know my rights."

Another minute and he would be out of control. She motioned for Bernard, who either didn't see her gesture or did and decided to ignore her. Jack now stood between her and the "panic button" under her desk. She could always leave through the door, but then she'd face having to restrain him out on the floor. That was the last thing Miranda needed to see. She decided to try to bluff him herself. "The hospital has lawyers, too, Mr. Reynolds," she said, meeting his gaze. "I consulted with one before you came this morning. The fact is, we need to evaluate the home situation before we can allow Miranda to return to you."

Jack struggled to maintain control. Who did she think she was, this woman who wanted to *evaluate* him, as though she were the judge and jury? Evaluate him! He had cared for Miranda all her life, by himself since Laurie had left. He was Miranda's father, for Christ's sake. There was no one in the world who loved her more, or took better care of her than he did. Why, anyone could tell her that. *Miranda* could tell her that. He struggled to keep his voice calm. "I know my rights," he repeated. "You can't keep her in this place against her will. She's not a danger to herself and she's sure as hell not a danger to others, and I'm a damn good father. So let me take her home."

Abby thought of all the times she had longed to steal Sarah from the doctors who had held her daughter hostage to their medicines and tubes—for her own good, of course. *Let me take her home,* she had begged, and they had stood there and said no. Just as she was saying now. How he must hate her, she thought, knowing the cold, impersonal rage of the powerless toward those with power. But she did have the power now, and she was determined to protect her patient. She was not going to lose this girl.

"I was hoping we could avoid this," she said, "but I need to tell you now that we believe your daughter is mentally ill. Our lawyers are prepared to go to court if necessary, to make sure that she gets the care she needs." She thought of Tom, and adopted his bravado. "If you choose to go that route and lose, your daughter could be declared a 'Person in Need of Supervision.' You could lose your parental rights. And none of us wants that to happen." *Well, almost none,* she thought.

Jack could feel blood pounding in his head. This bitch! She had a lot of nerve, telling him that he could not take adequate care of his daughter. He wondered if she had any children herself, if she had any idea of the work it took to raise a child. His eyes scanned her hands, noted a diamond-studded band on her ring finger. So she was married, at least. Maybe she was infertile—maybe that was it. Maybe she got a kick out of stealing other people's children because she had none of her own. But he knew the law. No judge in the world would hear all that he had done for Miranda, would hear from Miranda how much she wanted to be at home with him, and force her to live with strangers. He almost laughed at the doctor's naïveté. Really, it would be funny if it weren't so pathetic.

As he thought of Miranda talking to the doctor, he felt a sudden flash of fear. What might Miranda have told her? Yes, she was his daughter, but she was still a female. Who knew what lies she might be capable of, what fantasies might hatch in her evil little brain? His eyes narrowed. Maybe Laurie had gotten in touch with her. Maybe that bitch had cooked up a plot with this doctor to get Miranda away from him. If Laurie was around, he wouldn't put it past her. He wouldn't put anything past any of them. So the first job would be to win Miranda back. And he'd have to do it soon, before court, before she was able to mouth off God knows what to the judge, where it would be his word against hers.

Of course, he was the adult. He was the sane one. The doctor was going to testify that Miranda was crazy. It was beautiful. No matter what she said, it would just be the ramblings of a crazy girl. He almost laughed out loud. The doctor was going to play right into his hands. Her little plot would be no match for his. It was like a chess game, only he could see moves and moves ahead, all the way down to the checkmate, while this witch doctor remained focused on the pawn.

He smiled benignly at Abby. "Fine. If that's the way you want it, I'll see you in court."

Surprised by his easy acquiescence, Abby nodded briefly. "All right. I'll call you tomorrow to let you know when the hearing's been scheduled."

"Very good." Until then, he'd play along. That was the way to go. They wanted to evaluate him? Fine. Just let them try to say he had abused or neglected his daughter. They could test her in any subject they wanted. She was way ahead of grade level on all of them. There was no other father in the world who did the things for his kid that he did for Miranda. Just let them try to say he was an unfit parent. It was laughable. No sense butting heads. He could wait for the hearing.

He brushed roughly against Abby as he walked through the door. "Now if you'll just get my daughter . . ."

"Of course," Abby said, following him back out into the hall. "I'm sure you'll want to have a nice visit."

Miranda walks out of her room and sees her father and the tall woman talking at the end of the hall. They are standing under a light, and their hair is shining like fire. As she watches, they grow taller and taller and the other people fade away. Natalie is a shadow near the wall, and the nurses, the thin boy, the girl with the pimple-scarred face are small and dim. The woman is as tall as her father. They stand eye to eye, speaking in the light, and Miranda is awed by their power. That was the test! Her father was lost because he meant to be lost. He wanted her to find her mother and Miranda did find her and then her mother unkilled him and now they are all there together, the three of them, a family. She wants to laugh and skip, and she hugs herself to keep the laughter inside because she knows it is a secret and she is not supposed to know. Of course they did not kill her. Her mother would not let them. As long as she is here she will be safe, as she was safe at home. Her parents are talking, close together, face-to-face in the light, and the sun is warm, and later there will be applesauce for lunch. She walks toward them, smiling, and, smiling, they beckon her on.

Chapter Nine

Miranda sits on her bed, eating an orange that she has saved from dinner. She sucks at each section, feeling the juice wash over her tongue before she bites into the flesh. When she is done, she piles the skin neatly on a napkin beside her bed. Her father has told her that she will be going home soon to live with him again, and that she will not have to stay in this place anymore. *This is not a place to be safe in*, he said. *Don't listen to what they tell you.* Miranda remembers his voice and his face when he talked to her, and suddenly she understands that he is frightened. Her father is afraid.

She licks the sticky juice off her fingers. Her mother must be very powerful to frighten her father. He was never afraid of her not-mother, never. It is good to think that her father is frightened. It makes her glad, but she does not know why, and then she feels sorry, because it is a bad thought, and she knows her father should not feel afraid. She does not feel afraid, although her father says it is not a safe place, because the doctor says it is a safe place, and she has oranges to eat, as she did at home. At home there is her father and the safe, still, quiet, dead days, but her mother is here and the days are noisy and bumpy and filled with dead-beaver girls, but the snakes are gone. Dr. Cohen says that there are no snakes on the street, and Miranda understands that for her there are none, because her power can keep them away. But her father did see the snakes. He must be weaker than the doctor. Perhaps the doctor will keep her here until she can go home with her mother and her father. It will be good to be all together, the three of them, father, mother, Miranda. The doctor says maybe Miranda can go to school. The doctor has breasts and she is safe. Miranda bounces gently on her bed.

Abby sat at a table in Polson's Café, waiting for Tom. She was habitually early, always spurring herself to hurry so as not to keep others waiting, not to miss anything. She always had to wait, of course, but waiting was not so bad. She liked the tickle of anticipation and the sense of settling in, like a lioness hiding in the sandy-colored grass, watching the animals gather at the water hole as she picked one out for her prey. In fact, she had been anticipating this luncheon since she made plans with Tom the week before. His image had floated in her mind through meetings and subway rides, crowding out thoughts and leaving her distracted and vaguely guilty. She was too old to have a crush, she told herself, but still, she felt her foot jiggle nervously under the table as she waited for him to come.

The restaurant, in the atrium of an office building, was cool and light, crowded with suntanned men in summer suits and crisp striped shirts, and women with shiny hair and bare bronzed arms. She sat behind an enormous menu, scanning the choices, although she already knew what she'd order. As she sipped her iced tea, she listened to the cacophony of voices and laughter and clattering silverware and enjoyed the feeling that, although alone, she was waiting for a man in a summer suit to come and join her, too.

When Tom arrived she saw him first, watched him glance at his own face in the mirror at the bar and reach up with his hand to smooth his wavy brown hair. She smiled, enjoying the rush of power his gesture brought her. His suit was olive, and he wore a patterned red tie knotted loosely around his neck atop his light blue shirt. She saw him scan the room and reached up with her arm to signal him home. He found her with his eyes and smiled, returning her wave before nodding to the hostess and coming to join her.

"Sorry I'm late. I couldn't get off the phone."

Abby smiled at him. He looked incredibly young and fresh, like Ben, almost. She resisted the urge to reach out and ruffle his hair. How old was he, anyway? Twenty-eight? Twenty-nine? Thirty at the most. Only seven or eight years younger than she. God, she felt old. "You're not late, really. I was just early."

She ordered a large Greek salad with a side of pita, and he ordered a hamburger and a diet Coke. The waiter left, and there was a silence in the noisy room. Abby reached for a breadstick as Tom sipped his water. "So did you hear?" Abby asked, making conversation. "You know the new kid on the ward, Johnny Sewall?" Tom nodded. "He's decided that Johnny's just his pseudonym, and now he wants everyone to call him by his 'real' name."

"Which is?"

"Ubiquitous God," she said.

Tom choked on his water. "That's great. Let's hope he requests a commitment hearing. I've never been able to bring a case against God before."

Abby remembered Miranda, the ostensible focus of their lunch. That would be a safe topic. "Speaking of commitment hearings, what's happening with the hearing for Miranda Reynolds?"

Tom shrugged. "Not much. We're set for next week. Tuesday, I think. I'll have to check my book."

Abby finished chewing her breadstick and swallowed, feeling sharp crumbs lingering against her gums. She took a sip of water and rubbed her tongue over the surface of her teeth. Six more days to convince Jack that leaving his daughter with her was the right thing to do, or they'd have to let a judge decide. "What are our chances?"

"Honestly? Not great. It's going to be hard to argue that she's a danger to herself or to others, when she's never shown the remotest sign of aggression or impulsivity. And as far as having Daddy declared unfit—he *has* cared for her all her life."

Abby was angry. "Cared for her? From what little I can piece together, he seems to have kept her caged up like an animal. He's a real piece of work."

"I'm not saying he should be nominated for father of the year. But the threshold is pretty high in these cases."

"Yeah, but he's crazy. A real borderline. I wouldn't be surprised if he'd had a few psychotic breaks of his own."

"Look, I'm on your side here and I'll do my best. But

you asked me what I think our chances are, and I'm telling you that I don't think they're good."

Their food came. Abby eyed her plate without appetite while Tom squirted a pool of ketchup onto his burger and another onto his plate near a large pile of fries. "Want my pickle?" he asked.

Abby laughed. "I bet you say that to all the girls."

"Of course not. I've never offered my pickle to anyone before."

"Yeah, right."

"Do you want it or not?"

"Well, sure. Thanks." She paused. "I wish you'd told me all this earlier. You should have heard me talking to Mr. Reynolds. I made it sound like he had no case."

He took a bite of his hamburger and chewed thoughtfully. "That's not necessarily a bad thing. Maybe it'll scare him off. And I know that I said I liked our chances, but that was before Big Daddy surfaced. With a parent around and wanting her out, well, you know . . ."

"But you should see this parent. He's psycho. Really. As crazy as any kid on the unit."

"Has he abused her?"

Abby bit into a tomato and shook her head. "No. At least, she hasn't said anything."

Tom looked at her face, then cupped her hand with his own. "Don't worry," he said. "We'll think of something."

"That's what I say when I'm really out of ideas."

Tom laughed. "Oh, no. Busted. But since neither of us has any ideas at the moment, do you think we can talk about something else?"

Abby felt a momentary blip of irritation. "You mean, besides work? What else is there?"

"I don't know. Seen any good movies lately?"

She thought of Michael, who had recently suggested that they get a sitter and get out for a change, and felt a brief flicker of guilt. She would not tell him about this lunch, and she would not talk to Tom about Michael. Instead, she shook her head no. "I lead a boring life," she said. So he told her about a movie he'd seen, and then they gossiped about hospital politics and who was sleeping with whom, talked about books and plans for vacations later in the summer, and it was only toward the end of lunch, as Abby was sopping up the puddle of honey vinaigrette dressing with the last piece of pita, that she emerged from herself enough to realize that the part of her that since Sarah's death had seemed to hover near the ceiling watching the rest of her live her life had miraculously delved back inside her, and that for the duration of this one lunch on this one particular day, she had at last felt whole.

As they left the cool of the restaurant for the humid air outside, it felt to Abby that they were walking into a giant mouth. "God, it's disgusting out here."

"It's summer," Tom said. "It's supposed to be hot."

"Says who? Where I grew up—"

"And where was that?"

"Well, here, actually." Tom laughed, and Abby went on. "But we spent our summers on Martha's Vineyard." She thought of her vacation, now only two months away. She was no longer sure she even wanted to go.

" 'We spent our summers on Martha's Vineyard,' " Tom

repeated, his voice a parody of a New England accent. "You sound like someone from a nineteenth-century novel."

"Don't kid yourself," Abby told him. "I am someone from a nineteenth-century novel." She began to cough. "Did I happen to mention my consumption?"

They were almost at the hospital. Tom took hold of her arm. "This is fun," he said. "Let's not go back. Let's play hooky." He paused. "We could go for a walk in the park."

"You've got to be kidding! It's, like, a thousand degrees out here."

"Oh, come on. Feel that air! Soon it's going to be winter, and you'll wish for a day like today."

"I think not," Abby said as she mentally reviewed her commitments for the afternoon: a two o'clock staff meeting, a three o'clock class on the borderline adolescent, a four o'clock supervision, and then three hours of private-practice patients in the evening. "I have to get back," she said. "I've got a staff meeting in twenty minutes."

"Which will be a total loss if you're not there. Am I right?"

"Well, yes, kind of."

"A complete flop without your invaluable contribution."

Abby felt the warmth of the sun beating down and suddenly remembered summer as it had been in her childhood, how time seemed to widen and stretch like a yawn. She felt the pull of Tom's invitation like the rush of the ocean tide, the waves and shells and sand straining against her ankles, tugging her into its undulating depths. "I could be a few minutes late, I guess."

He smiled and they turned together away from the hospital and walked across Fifty-ninth Street toward Central Park. As they passed by the statue of Christopher Columbus, Tom darted ahead and bought Abby a frozen lemonade, which he presented to her with a flourish, as though he were offering something of great value. "Mmmm, thanks," she said, grateful for the cool, sweet slush, which she sucked in freezing bites off a long-handled plastic spoon, as well as for the distraction that the act of eating itself presented, a talisman to hold in her hand, so it was no longer free to be held by him.

The park tableau was as vivid and dappled as a painting by Seurat. Everywhere Abby looked, there seemed to be people moving to the rhythms of the summer day. Men and women in tight black pants swooped and glided around them on Rollerblades like a flock of large, ungainly birds. On the grass, grown tall and prickly, smooth bronzed bodies lay nearly naked, baking in the sun. "Doesn't anybody go to work anymore?" Abby wondered aloud. "Who are all these people, anyway?"

"Who are we?" answered Tom.

"*We* are responsible people, ignoring our responsibilities," said Abby. "But at least we have responsibilities to ignore."

"You're right. They're bums, the lot of them. They should all go to—"

"Law school?"

"God spare them."

They kept walking, burrowing deeper into the park. Abby was suddenly conscious of Tom's smell, a sweet male scent of sweat and aftershave. He had taken off his jacket and rolled up his sleeves, and his arms looked strong and brown. "I know," he said. "Let's go on the carousel."

"The carousel!"

"Sure. Come on. It'll be fun."

In the distance, Abby could hear the plink-plunk of the music, tin-canned strains of turn-of-the-century songs, songs her grandparents used to sing, *Daisy, Daisy, give me your answer true,* sounds that used to send Sarah racing ahead down the path yelling *Pleasepleaseplease* as Abby trotted behind and laid down a dollar for a three-minute ride that used to cost a quarter when *she* was a girl. She remembered her own childhood like a shadow as it stood, more real than any memory, next to Sarah in the line, struggled with her through the crush of children pressing up to the horses, ran with her past manes forever flying in the wind to the horse that had been both their favorite, a wild roan stallion with a saddle in the shape of a lion on his back. Abby could feel the weight of Sarah as she lifted her up onto her horse, heavier each year and then, much later, heartbreakingly light. She had not been on the carousel in two years. Michael took Ben now, or her parents did, or Lolly.

But Tom did not know about Sarah. When he looked at the horses flying by, he saw people, not ghosts. She wondered what he saw when he looked at her, and knew that whatever it was, he was spared the sight of the biblical Leah crying endlessly for her lost children. "No," she said. "I get nauseous on those things."

"Suit yourself, spoilsport."

Spoilsport indeed, lady of doom, a walking rain cloud

on a sunny day. Michael had told her once that she seemed to sweat sorrow, letting it ooze out of her pores until she was covered with its film. Two years later, and still she reeked of it. *This is not who I am,* she wanted to say, but the words would not come. Perhaps they were no longer even true. Sometimes she felt that, in the fullness of this fecund world, all that was precious to her lay locked in a metal box and that she lacked the key. But at other times she felt it was she who was locked in the box when the one with the key had gone forever.

Her frozen lemonade had melted to syrup so sweet that it stung her throat as she swallowed. "Let's go back," she said. "It's getting late."

He looked at her, puzzled and annoyed. "Right."

They walked in silence through the park, emerging from the trees into the noise and heat of Columbus Circle. "So you'll call Jack Reynolds?" Abby asked. "Try to scare him off the hearing?"

Tom curled his hands into claws. "I am a scary guy, apparently."

"Funny."

"I'll give him a call," Tom said. "But don't get your hopes up."

Somehow, the silence between them had turned awkward, filled in Abby's mind with words unsaid that clogged her throat and made speaking impossible. As they neared the hospital, Tom suddenly announced that he had a quick errand to run. Abby was dubious—he hadn't mentioned errands before—but she felt grateful that he was sparing them the sweaty joint entrance, almost an hour late, into the hospital and the awkward parting at the door. "Thanks for lunch," he said. "I'll let you know what happens with Reynolds."

"Please do." He set off down the street as Abby stood on the corner, waiting for the light to change. When she turned around, he was gone, having disappeared around the corner, and she was left standing there, uncertain how to feel, with relief and regret shimmering before her in the brutal midday sun.

Chapter Ten

The air-conditioned cold comes off Miranda's window like a bird and nests inside her bones. She feels her blood thicken and slow inside her veins and remembers the story her father read her of the man who froze in the snow because he could not light a fire. Her father is there and he is talking to her and his voice is saying, "Don't worry, Miri. Soon I will take you home."

The cold hurts her bones. She sees her silent room in her mind and the silent river of days and then her mother is there with her in her mind and she does not want to lose her. Her eyes feel wet and then her voice is in the room, rushing out of her like vomit as she tries to suck it back. "No. I don't want to go."

"What?" His voice echoes in her mind, as though her brain is nothing but a vast canyon. "I can take you home, you know. I will take you home."

And then she hears a higher voice again, rushing ahead to do battle with the deep one. She thinks the voice is hers.

In her ears it sounds faint, but surprisingly strong. "No. I don't want to go."

Her father looks at her. "I don't like the way you're behaving, young lady. I don't like it at all."

She drops her head and watches her feet going *tap, tap, tap* against the floor. Inside herself she feels a strong smile. She watches as her father abruptly gets up and leaves the room, but when he is gone she turns to stone.

Inside her bed there is a hurricane. The roiling of the waves makes her feel that she will be sick, and the noise of the wind swirling around her ears makes her afraid. Yet she knows the voices, knows they are neither monsters nor gods but her and her father, fighting each other, and what scares her most is not his anger but the fear on his face, because she knows it is a fear of her. *I can take you home, you know. No. I don't want to go. I don't want to go. I. Want. To stay.* Her mother's face is in her mind and she can feel herself wanting and the feeling is scary, too, because it is new and feels too much like hunger, which is never scary because her father always gives her food, but this wanting is like a lion's open mouth inside, red and angry, and she is not sure what will fill it. Shivering, she forces herself to look inside the lion's mouth, where the teeth gleam white and sharp, and she knows that if she cannot give it what it wants, it will devour her instead.

Outside herself the hurricane grows stronger and then the rocking is too much and she knows she will be sick. Throwing off the covers, she runs to the bathroom and retches into the toilet, vomiting up a putrid brown spew that she knows is the essence of herself. "Daddy!" she calls. "Daddy, I'm sick!" But he does not come.

They will help you at the hospital, says his voice inside her mind. *That is where you want to stay. And you're right. You're sick. You belong in a hospital. They help sick people there.* His laugh is ugly in her ears and she forces herself to look into the filthy water with the bits of half-digested bread and chunks of unchewed carrot and thinks, *Yes, this is you. This is what you are.*

Her tears plop into the bowl and she watches the ripples as the stench of herself is carried back inside through her nose. *I want to stay.* The words are inside her, too, like rancid cream inside a pastry. *I want. No. Want not. Waste not want not.* Her father does not want her to want for anything. He tells her that. *Remember, Miranda, you do not want for anything. I will give you all that you need.* Squeezing her eyes shut, she grabs the flesh of her stomach in her hand and grips it tight to stop the wanting, but it is a part of her now and she can neither vomit it up nor push it out.

She stands up, flushes the toilet, and rinses her mouth, then brushes her teeth till her breath smells like mint. Standing before the door, she pauses to look at herself in the mirror. Eyes, nose, mouth, all swollen and moist. Inside her eyes she can see her mother. She is silent and still, but she is there. *You are stronger than you think,* she says, and then she is gone. In the mirror, Miranda's eyes are empty and her face is as smooth and hard as a mask. She tries to leave her body, but there is something blocking her way. Frightened, she crouches inside herself, willing herself to consume as little space as possible as she quietly lets her hand open the door.

In the hall she hears her father's voice; he is talking to her mother. His voice is angry and rough in her ears, but he is not talking to her and she makes the words go far away. Her father does not get angry at Miranda, because Miranda is a good girl, but if he ever did get angry at her . . . *I will be good,* she thinks. She goes into the dayroom. The wind has stopped, and the air is hot and wet. She sits on a chair and looks at her toes, but they do not take her away and she is afraid. Trapped, she begins to move, slowly at first and then faster and faster, drumming her fingers on the rough fabric, then pounding with her feet, and finally spinning, faster and faster, watching the walls and books and lights spin with her until they are swallowed up inside her and she falls on the floor, huddled into herself, feeling the world spin as the arms reach out to grab her and she curls inside herself and when the snake bites she does not feel it at all.

Jack watched his daughter spin around the room like a crazy person, and for the first time, he felt afraid. They had done something to her all right. He had come for her as soon as he could, but it was already too late. He had told her she could go, that he would take her home, and the doctor had said no. And now this performance. She was trying to screw him, just like they all did. She could act crazy with the best of them—he'd have to admit that. And if a judge saw the act he'd just witnessed, well, hell, he'd be the one in a psycho ward if he tried to say that she was sane.

"Mr. Reynolds?"

He spun around to see Miranda's doctor. Ready to gloat, no doubt. "I can see what a great job y'all are doing," he said bitterly. "She's looking *so much* better than she did at home."

The look on her face was pathetic. "I'm sorry," she said, her voice oh-so-soft and sincere. "She's really never done that before. Do you know of anything that might have upset her?"

Jack snorted. "I have no idea." Like he was supposed to know what the hell they'd done to destroy his little girl. But he had to admit, whatever they'd done, they were winning, for now. He looked her right in the face, and told her: "You won the battle, but don't think that you won the war."

"Sorry?" she said.

"You heard me."

Again that fake smile, dripping concern. How he'd love to punch it off her face. "We're all on the same side, aren't we? We all want to help Miranda."

We all want to help Miranda. "Well, you're doing a great job so far."

The doctor lady began to walk away, motioning for him to follow. Dirty kids who lined the hallway parted for them as they passed. The air smelled thick with grease and burned bread. It was almost dinnertime, and what would Miranda get to eat? Shot up with drugs, she'd be lying on a bed somewhere, vulnerable to any fruitcake that happened by. And the place was full of fruitcakes. No, it *was* a fruit-cake. Full of nuts and fruits! He laughed to himself. That was a good one. He'd have to tell Miranda when he'd finally gotten her home and deprogrammed. He'd heard on TV about kids who were brainwashed into cults. If you had the money, you could hire these rescue guys to steal them back and get their minds straightened out again. That was one thing he could do.

He walked into her office and she closed the door behind them. God, he was beginning to hate this room, with its soft, squishy cushions and curvy pastel paintings. It was like his mother's room. A girl's place. No place for him.

"So I've been thinking," Abby said at last. "I know you're worried about Miranda's schooling, but I think it's clear she's not quite ready to go home yet."

"Clear as mud," Jack answered.

Abby picked up a pen and began to doodle on a yellow pad. "Have you asked her what she wants?"

Jack glared at her, eyes blazing. "Now why should I do that?" he said. "She's *crazy*, right? So how is she supposed to know what she wants?" Calm, calm, he told himself. "I am her father," he said. "It's for me to decide what's best for her."

Abby nodded agreement. "Of course," she said. "But to address your concern about schooling, I just wanted you to know that we have a school program here, for kids Miranda's age. In fact, as soon as they're ready, all the kids on the unit attend. Even when they're well enough to leave the hospital, a lot of them still continue on in the school during the day. It's a great program. Small classes, excellent teachers. They have therapy, learn coping skills—along with their academics, of course."

Jack could hear it in his mind: the noises of crazy children, laughing, screaming, crying, spinning around the room like Miranda had done. He could just see her there, his Miranda, surrounded by all that chaos, his daughter, who was used to, who *needed*, the quiet of her own room to keep her thoughts in order. It was perfect. He would cooperate, oh yes. No one, not Miri, not this Cohen lady, would be able to say he had not tried his best. But she would hate it. After a few more weeks in that place, she'd want to go home, all right. Hell, she'd beg to go home; she'd give up this stupid crazy act and tell the judge all sane and sure that she wanted to be with her dad. And the judge, benevolent and wise, would agree. It was brilliant.

"You know, that sounds good," he said, trying to suppress his glee.

Dr. Cohen looked surprised. "All right, then." She paused. "So does that mean you don't want to go ahead with the hearing?"

Ha! He was foiling her little plan. She had *wanted* the hearing. Of course she had. And now she'd see that she'd gotten the little crazy act together for nothing. Oh, it was beautiful. "Not just yet," he said, smiling. "I guess it is best if she stays. For now." He got up. "If you don't mind, I think I'll go check on her."

"Well, sure," Abby said, watching in stunned silence as he got up and walked through the door.

We won! she thought. *We actually won.* She could not wait to tell Tom.

Chapter Eleven

A bby sat with Michael in their bedroom, pretending to read, as her mind replayed her lunch with Tom and a feeling of excitement prickled her skin like a sunburn. The room was full of noises, but her thoughts drowned out sound. From time to time, Michael's hand reached out to stroke her thigh, his eyes never moving from his page. Under his caress her skin felt numb, his touch annoying as a mosquito. With effort, she resisted the urge to brush his hand away.

She allowed herself to be borne along by the sensations filling her mind: the warmth of the summer sun and the cold of frozen lemonade, the brushes of skin against skin, the tingling rush of feeling that had stung her body like prickly heat. All the feelings and pictures and words came in seconds, layered rather than linear, so that it might have taken hours to describe them. And on top of it all, in Abby's mind, was the knowledge of this, and the certainty that to explain even a part, you would need music rather than words. In the instant that thought crossed her mind she became aware that she had been humming to herself all day, and only now remembered the words that fitted the tune: *She's got a ticket to ride, she's got a ticket to ri-I-ide.*

But what was she riding to? she wondered. She pictured Tom's hands as they had waved before him at lunch, defining a point, and found herself wondering how they would feel against her breasts. She wanted a ticket there— that was all: a ticket to another life where there was noise and color and something besides a silent man reading beside her and stroking her the way one might stroke a cat. A life where nothing bad had happened yet. Michael would never have to know, she thought to herself. And if he knew, would he really even care?

Monogamy had been easy for her. She did not need lovers or flowers or clandestine dinners in seedy hideaways. She did not miss variety in bed, where Michael's familiar touch knew exactly how to gratify her without her even trying. But the feeling she had now, the strange, wide-open eagerness of beginning something new—marriage had frozen and buried it, and the feeling she had now was like a thaw. She remembered the feeling from childhood: coming in from sledding with frozen fingers, running them gingerly under warm water, enduring the painful burn and tingle until normal sensation returned. There was pain in this thaw, too, especially if she let herself think of Michael. The trick, of course, was not to think.

Michael finished his chapter and closed the book. His eyes followed a baseball game on television as the announcer's voice explained why the man on first should not be trying to steal, and why the first baseman was playing too close to the bag. On cue, the batter slapped the pitch through the infield hole. There was a crack and a cheer, and the man on first began to run, pressing forward with his body until he slid safely into third.

"Yes!" Michael said.

"What's the score?"

Michael shrugged. "Mets are winning for a change. Three–two, I think. I haven't really been paying attention."

The air conditioner shuddered into silence. Abby waited a moment and then looked down at her book.

"We should take Ben to a game," Michael said.

The thought of dragging Ben to Shea Stadium on the subway, of sitting in a stadium entertaining her son while Michael watched the game, exhausted her. "He'd get bored after two innings."

"Yeah. You're right." He turned back to the television, annoyed. The silence stretched and deepened around him, and she watched as he receded into it like a ship sailing toward the horizon. Hell, they couldn't even fight anymore, it seemed.

She began absently twirling her ring around her finger and then stopped, forcing herself to look at the object itself, the tiny diamonds embedded like stars in the golden band. They had bought it on a cool spring day, and in the August heat of their wedding it had been barely big enough to fit over her swollen finger. She remembered the long pause, a hush marked by whispers and giggles, as Michael had struggled to push it over her knuckle. And finally, after he had gotten it on and they had been duly pronounced husband and wife, having hugged and kissed for so long that a louder wave of laughter had erupted, he had turned to her and said, *You'll never be able to take it off, you know.* And she had answered, *Don't worry. I won't ever want to.*

"We could take him to a game if you want," Abby conceded.

"No, you're right. He'd just get bored."

The silence settled around them again, drowning out noise. She thought of Miranda, and how the silence in their sessions sometimes seemed to take on weight and form, holding them in its gentle embrace. But this silence was different. It felt heavy, pressing down upon her. *This must be what it's like to freeze to death,* she thought. She could imagine herself just giving in to the silence, letting it wrap itself around her throat so that she never spoke again. Once, she had treated a little girl who had chosen to be mute. It had been one of Abby's successes, actually. She had cured her by joining her in the silence, knowing her without speech and without demands until the girl felt safe enough to speak without fear. Abby remembered sitting with the child through dozens of silent hours, awed by the power of saying absolutely nothing, until the end of the session, when her own voice saying that their time was up seemed both foreign and somehow deeply wrong.

"What do you want to do this weekend?" she asked. Her voice sounded strange in her ears.

Without looking up, Michael shrugged.

There's no need to sulk, Abby thought. "I said we could go to a ball game, if you want."

"No."

"Then what? A picnic in the park?"

"Sure. That sounds like fun."

Michael, I'm sorry, she thought, but the words would not come.

She got up. "I'm going to get myself a snack," she said. "Want anything?"

"Nope," he said. "Nothing at all."

She felt a sharp burning of guilt in her chest. He had been trying, as he so often did, with more strength than she possessed, to bench-press their life back on track. It was he who thought to take Ben to the movies, who brought out the plastic bat and Wiffle ball and taught him how to hit. And she could barely summon the energy to smile.

She resolved yet again to try harder, and when, later that night, he reached for her in bed, she did not turn away. She felt his erection grow against her bottom, his hand reaching up to rub her nipples. Slowly she felt herself relax against him as he kissed her neck, began to want his weight over her, inside her.

"Wait," she said, reaching for her diaphragm.

"No, don't." He held her close. "You feel so good."

"Michael." She slipped away from his embrace. Taking her diaphragm from its pink clamshell case, she quickly squirted jelly inside and slipped it into place. "All set." He kissed her neck, his warm breath against her flesh making her squirm.

"Do you think we'll ever have another child?" he asked. Abby felt her flesh go dead. His hands against her flank might have been stroking a tree.

"I don't know."

She rolled onto her back and pulled him on top of her,

kissing his mouth into silence, but the sweet sense of desire was gone. He entered her, and she moved her hips to his rhythm while her mind was far away, imagining a baby cradled in her arms. By the time he came, she was close to tears. "I love you," he said, and she echoed his words, turning her head so that her tears would land on her pillow instead of his shoulder. She *had* wanted to make love—that was the funny part. She wanted so much to be part of him again, part of something, someone. God, she was lonely. They were like two satellites in space, trying to dock without speaking, one into the other, unable to coordinate movements so that one jerked up while the other swung down, and each was left to drift into infinity alone.

"Michael," she said.

"Mmmm?"

"Can we talk a bit?"

"Sure."

She was silent for a long time. In the darkness, she saw Sarah, cheeks flushed red as Jell-O from the cortisone, arm tethered to a long plastic tube that carried fluid into her veins. She smelled slightly sour, like milk gone bad. Moon face, Abby had called her, with skin as cool and thin as a new piece of paper.

"Do you remember—" she began, and was met by Michael's rhythmic breathing. He had fallen asleep. Of course. Even in the months after Sarah's death, he had been able to fall asleep almost instantly, while she had been condemned to lie there with dry open eyes staring at the ceiling, listening to peace and oblivion beside her. Lying there, eyes closed, snoring slightly, he seemed walled in by his skin, separate, a stranger. Her eyes moved down the sharp curve of his neck, the black fur that covered his chest. The sheet rose like a shroud against the curve of his hip, and she could feel without touching the slightly rough, dimpled skin beneath. "Michael," she whispered, but he did not stir. And then she hated him. She wanted to take her pillow and press it over his open mouth until he choked and died. But rage took too much energy. It wasn't his fault. It wasn't anybody's fault. It was only a deadness inside her, which left her looking at his back in the sepia room as though it were an old photograph that hung on a wall, long after its colors had faded.

Chapter Twelve

The noises of the others are loud, but they no longer frighten Miranda. She sees them with their staring eyes, hears their snorts and groans and sighs, and knows that they are nothing more than people who will not hurt her. She is here, waiting for her mother (not-mother), who will come soon. Her father will come, too. He will clutch her hand and then let go. She smiles inside herself because she knows that he is the one who is afraid. The smile does not show on her face. It makes him angry, her strong smile, and she has learned to smile it only where it cannot be seen. She has learned many things, she thinks, and she hears a voice inside her mind: *You have a lot to learn, little girl. A lot to learn.*

Miranda watches through the window, sees the people walking along the crowded sidewalk. Her mother had swum into that current of motion, had gotten swept away. She listens for her mother's footsteps, but they are lost in the hum of traffic. Worried now, she stamps her feet—stomp, stomp, stomp on the floor—and calms at once as the sound comes into her ear. Satisfied, she hums to herself, and it feels like closing a door.

She is waiting for her mother, who will take her to her first day of school. Her mother is late. Miranda goes to the hallway, where she sits in a chair and rubs her fingers against the smooth red vinyl. *Look around*, her father says in her mind. *This is what you wanted. This is what you got.*

Miranda looks around. Her eyes pass over the black and white squares of linoleum, the feet in scuffed shoes shuffling by. There is a window inside that is covered with glass, and the woman in the window has a smile that is not strong or scared but maybe kind. *Beware the kindness of strangers,* she thinks. *Beware of the dog. Beware. Be where. Be where?* And although she is here, is where she wanted to be, it no longer feels as it did in her mind. As though in the getting, the wanting itself had changed, into a feeling that frightened her. Her heart beats too fast and her stomach hurts. She chews on the inside of her cheek, clenches down hard, tastes the tinny tang of blood. *Let's go,* she wants to say, but the wanting itself holds danger. *This is what you wanted,* her father says, and his eyes are not kind at all. *I want to go home.* But the words are inside her and she has forgotten how to speak.

When Abby comes at last, Miranda smells her soap-clean scent and hears the *click-click* of her shoes but does not open her eyes. The flute voice is in the air, but Miranda wills the words into music and begins to rock. Her father's voice first halts the music, then rides along with it, like a dolphin coasting on the crest of a wave, and then she is a dolphin, breaking through the water and laughing at the salt-sweet drops that shimmer in the sun. The water is cold, but the sun is warm. It feels good on her dolphin skin.

Her dolphin fins wave good-bye as she turns flips in the salty ocean spray. Her dolphin friends surface and swim around her in a circle, calling in a language that sounds like a song. There are mermaids under the sea, they say, and they want her to come and be their queen. Feeling strong and safe, she opens her eyes to see Abby standing silent before her. Miranda forces herself to look at her and finds that the person they have sent her is not who she remembers and not who she wants. The fear comes again, hard and fast, and she dives back below the waves into the silent world of water. Her eyes dart upward again through the undulating layers of sea and sky to the blurry, slowly rocking figure above. She sees that the woman has grown skin between her fingers like webbing, and between her legs, fusing them into a tail. Of course. The mermaids have a queen already! The dolphins have tricked her, lured her into a trap. In a panic, she turns to swim away. The queen moves toward her, reaches to take her hand. Miranda screams and the fish scatter around her like sparks. The queen steps back and the words come out of her mouth in bubbles that float so quickly to the surface that Miranda cannot hear them. She watches the mouth opening and closing like a fish out of water, gasping for air, and suddenly she feels like laughing. This queen is not so powerful after all.

Abby stood before Miranda, watching her face, waiting for a signal to approach. The girl's soundless lips formed words she could not decipher. Silence had seemed to work best to calm her before, and so she stood silently for a long time, watching. Miranda's face was pale, as though all the color had drained inward, to the fantasies which must be absorbing her now, causing her eyelids to flutter in fear and her hands to clench and unclench against the arms of her chair. Her hair hung down her back in oily strings, and newly erupted pimples stained her forehead like a rash. Abby watched Miranda struggle with her anger and disappointment. *If only you could know,* she thought. *I am no less than I was before, and you found what you needed in me then. I am still here.*

She took a seat next to the girl, mirroring her posture, head down, feet restlessly scuffing against the floor. She tried to feel what the girl was feeling. Fear, of course, and a lifetime of disappointment, betrayal, abandonment, and solitude. Beneath it all she still saw hope, and tiny shards of health. She had made the connection once. She had only to make Miranda remember. She sat in silence, offering Miranda the gift she seemed to need more than any other. When the girl looked at her at last, she carefully refrained from smiling. "Let's go meet the others," she said softly.

Wordlessly, and without another glance, Miranda rose to follow.

Upstairs, the morning meeting was under way. Ten adolescents sat in a circle of folding chairs, with therapists marking north and south on the compass. Twenty eyes looked at the floor. On the dirty light blue walls, posters offered health and sanity "one day at a time" and exhorted readers to accept the things they could not change. The windows were caged with ancient metal screens and closed, muffling the sounds of the world outside. The loudest sound was the ticking of a clock on the wall. From north and south the two therapists, young women in their twenties dressed in long flowered skirts and short-sleeved sweaters, locked anxious eyes. "Come on, guys," exhorted North. "Someone must have an issue."

Finally one boy raised his head. His face was square and strong; his eyes were the color of well-steeped tea. Everything about him looked hard, angular, except for his mouth. That one feature, his wide, full lips, created a soft, almost feminine oasis in his face that Abby, for one, had yet to see mirrored in his demeanor. It was Freddy, expelled from school and freed from imprisonment on Tower Ten, sentenced to finish out the academic year in the Day Program. "I got an issue," he said in a loud, flat voice.

"Yes, Freddy?"

"This place sucks. That's my issue."

South sighed. "That's not an issue. That's a complaint."

"Is not."

Abby held her breath, waiting for the therapist to take the bait and say, "Is, too." Freddy would win then, but at the expense of any hope of their helping him, or Miranda, or any of them. Knowing that she should probably let the therapists handle the situation, she decided to burst in anyway.

"Hi, guys," she said, and the conversation stopped. Being "Big Mama" had its advantages. "This is Miranda. Some of you know her from Tower Ten. She's going to be joining us."

A few voices offered hellos.

"Hey," said Freddy. "Welcome. Just so you know, this place sucks."

Abby glared at him.

"Whatsamatter, Doc? Don't you believe in truth in advertising?"

Abby pulled two more chairs into the circle. As she worked, she replied offhandedly, "I believe in letting people decide for themselves." Not that it mattered, she thought. She was sure that wherever Miranda was, it was not in this room.

Miranda is far away on her horse, riding on a carousel and laughing to herself because the horses have children's faces and eyes the color of tea. She holds herself still as the music takes her round and round. When she closes her eyes, the music speeds up and the horses fly faster and faster until she grows dizzy and cries, "Stop!"

She opens her eyes and knows that her voice has not left her head, and she is glad. She sees that she is in a room full of children. Their faces are the ones she saw on the carousel, but their bodies have returned to human form. She wonders how she got here, then remembers her horse. He would never bring her to a place that was unsafe. They are ignoring her now, the others, and she listens to their voices blowing past her like wind. She is breathing, and the sound in her ears is like a horse's gentle snort. She can feel herself relax, and when she glances up at the tall, fiery mermaid queen, she sees that she is smiling.

Seeing-not-seeing, her eyes flicker strobelike across the faces in the circle. There is a boy with squinty eyes above a bulbous nose, a gargoyle face that threatens to swoop down and swallow her. Quickly she looks away, allowing herself to register a girl's face as thin and pointed as a fox's, or perhaps an elf's. She has green leprechaun eyes, which glitter like a pot of gold beneath a rainbow, offering magic that disappears like a mirage when she catches Miranda's glance. She turns instead toward the boy who is speaking. His voice sounds hard but hollow. He could shatter like glass, she thinks, and looks away because she knows that looks can kill. Beyond the therapist's smiling face she sees a round brownish circle with two kind eyes, partially hidden behind a growth of wavy hair. Natalie.

"Hey, Miranda," she says, and Miranda feels a wave of warmth. "It's good to see you, kid."

Despite herself, Miranda smiles.

"Oh," asks North, "do you two know each other? That's great."

Ignoring her, Natalie says, "We could play a game of checkers later, if you want to."

Natalie's voice feels like a kitten, rubbing against Miranda's cheek. "That would be nice," she says, and her smile feels real and safe.

Chapter Thirteen

Jack waited. He *bided his time.* He could be as patient as a panther stalking prey. He was nobody's fool. But it wasn't easy—he could tell them that. Not easy at all to smile at that doctor who had probably never cured anyone of so much as a headache in her life. Not easy to smile at Miranda, either, or pretend to ignore the way her body was becoming curvy and soft beneath those loose tops he had bought her.

Jack paced back and forth through his living room, his mouth chomping rhythmically on a stick of gum, releasing a flow of minty juice that stung his throat. It was hot in the apartment and sweat dampened his shirt beneath his arms and across his chest. Ten strong strides to the window and ten back to the door. He was a panther, all right, but they had caged him up. His daughter and the bitch had neutered him and caged him like an animal in the freaking zoo. He had never had a chance.

He paced and paced and felt his anger grow with each step, speeding his rhythm until he was practically running across the room. So now they had her in school, did they?

That was what they told him, anyway. Yeah, right. They thought he was so dumb, so uneducated, but he'd been to college. He knew all about school. He knew all about dorm rooms and boys sneaking into girls' beds, and girls inviting them in! He knew about that, all right. He knew about cigarettes smoked near open bathroom windows and smoke washed down with a Listerene gargle, and beer and probing tongues and groping fingers. . . .

As the momentum of his thoughts increased, his feet began to circle through the apartment until he reached Miranda's empty room and then he sputtered to a stop. His eyes scanned the room, quickly at first, like a hawk's seeking prey, and then more slowly, taking it in, seeing his child in her familiar childhood things. His eyes rested first on the neat rows of books on the shelves, arranged in perfect alphabetical order by title, just as he had asked, and then on the row of soft plush animals resting patiently above them. Her covers were pulled straight and tight on her bed, with the neat triangular folds at the corners that the army had taught him and that he had taught her. Above her bed was the poster of Babar and his cousin—what was his name?—taking flight in a shiny red airplane, their scarves streaming behind them in the clear blue sky. He had bought that for her when she was just a baby, really. He had been walking down Columbus Avenue— No, *they* had, he and Miranda's mother. . . .

He felt the anger, familiar and sharp, like the breaking of a bone, but in his mind the memory kept playing, wordless, like a silent movie scrolling across a screen: a man and a woman pushing a baby in a stroller, a baby who even at two loved the adventures of Babar, loved the picture of the elephant in his green coat and spats, loved the wedding of the king and the queen, loved the animals dancing in the dark and the newlywed couple staring out at the starry, starry night, a man and a woman and a baby walking down the street and seeing the poster in a store and walking through the door, laughing, just to see how much it cost, then turning, about to walk out again because it was so expensive, before being summoned back in by the man behind the counter, who sold it to them for half price because their baby was so beautiful. Arthur, damn it! That was the cousin's name. Arthur. He'd read the book enough times, he thought. He should at least remember that!

And all the other books she had loved, his daughter. *Goodnight Moon* and *Horton Hatches the Egg; Go, Dog. Go!* and *Are You My Mother?* Jack laughed roughly. He remembered that one, all right. The one where the mother bird leaves her baby in the nest while she goes gallivanting all about the town. Prophetic, that was what that one had been. And the baby bird is left, pathetic, wandering around to all the other animals, begging for his mommy, and getting slammed time and time again for his trouble. But he'd made sure that Miranda had never had to beg for care, never had to want for anything. After *she* left, he had vowed that he would care for Miranda so well that she would barely miss her . . . well, the woman who had *seemed* to be her mother. Because what the hell kind of mother left her kid? Even the bird in the stupid story had left only to get food, had gone only for a few minutes. It was an *accident* that the baby bird had hatched when the mother was away. And of course, in the end, the mother came back. *That* was what he called a mother. Not some salmon or trout, who deposited her eggs and then swam away before making sure that the babies had made it safely upstream. Which was why only, like, one in a hundred baby salmon made it! But Miranda was no fucking fish. She had a *father*. She had *him*.

And now this was the thanks he got.

After all he had done for her, she did not *want* to come home. Well, she could just see where wanting got you in this world. He had not *wanted* his dad to drink, had not *wanted* his mother to die, had not *wanted* the bitch to leave, if the truth be told (though he was glad she had now, goddamn it—it had turned out a lot better for them all in the end). And wasn't that the point? How could anyone ever really know what they wanted? Especially a kid. Wasn't that what parents were for? Come on! If kids wanted to eat candy all day, were parents supposed to let them?

In the beginning, he remembered, Miranda had not wanted to stay home without him. He remembered her whining, all day long, it seemed, for him to take her to school, take her to the library, take her to the park, like *Mommy* used to do. Oh, he could have smacked her for that one, he really could. Maybe he should have, even. But he never did. Had never hit her in her life, and he was proud of that. He'd given her better than what he'd had, just like a parent was supposed to do. He had reasoned with her, just like the books said, the ones *she* was always trying to make him read, like he didn't know how to raise his child without some fag Jew doctor telling him what to do. And pretty soon Miranda had understood. Daddy had to go to work, and it was safer to stay home because Daddy would be home soon. He was proud of how well they had managed together all these years, damn proud, proud of her and proud of himself, too.

And now she wanted to throw it all away.

That word again. *Want.* How could she possibly know what she wanted? How could anyone know? He remembered another story they had read together, about a princess who wanted the moon but was satisfied with a silver ball on a chain around her neck. Better that than the real moon, right? Who would want a million tons of barren rock in their room? Right? Right, Miranda? Right?

He knelt by her bed and pounded it with his fist, punching the mattress as hard as he could. "Right?" he screamed aloud. "Right? Right?" Beating his fist into her stomach and face and cunt as hard as he could, pounding, over and over.

And when it was over, he sat down on Miranda's bed and smoothed the covers with his hands as though her thin body were between them and he were stroking her back before sleep. She was still only a child, after all. His child. And he wanted her home.

Chapter Fourteen

It was almost like falling in love. Being with Miranda, watching her slow resurrection, made Abby feel full. As Miranda spoke or moved or sat silent, Abby studied her, breathed with her, learned the minutiae of her thoughts and the contours of her dreams. At times, the room seemed to expand around them so that the space in which they sat contained the whole of the world, and the hour they were together the whole of time. When they were apart, Abby carried the girl with her in her mind. She found herself talking about her, sharing anecdotes, trying to describe her essence but always falling short. Even at night, lying next to Michael as he slept, she saw Miranda's face as she stared up through the darkness.

Sometimes in their hour Miranda's speaking served to draw forth distant memories, for herself and Abby, too. Miranda would speak of her early years, years that held first moments and then remembered days of happiness she dimly saw but no longer seemed to own. As she spoke, Abby, too, found herself remembering, holding pictures in her mind of her own family as it had been before Sarah got sick, when they had romped with each other in full innocence of what hell lay ahead.

Sarah, she thought, had lived with an exclamation point. Where Abby's emotions were muted through the damper of her intellect, Sarah's had been expressed at full volume. They had sailed through the terrible twos, but at three, just after Ben was born, Sarah had turned truculent, always spoiling for a fight. Abby remembered Sarah in the taxi, on the ride home from the hospital with the new baby, methodically ripping every limb off of her doll. *What happened?* Michael had asked her one day. *You used to be such a nice girl.* And Abby remembered her daughter looking straight in his eyes as she said, *Well, Dad. People change.*

People change. People die. Ironic, thought Abby, that she and Michael had so often projected Sarah into the future. *She's going to be hell as a teenager,* they would laugh. *She'll be beating them off with a stick.* Abby had actually worried, at times, watching Sarah endlessly quarrel and make up with her best friend, Stephanie, that she would settle as an adult into one of those awful, bickering marriages that Abby had always scorned, that her selfishness and greed would metastasize in adulthood into a pernicious narcissism. *No one will be able to stand her!* Abby remembered saying to Michael one day after lobbying hard for boarding school. *Even I can't stand her.* But secretly, even then, Abby had envied Sarah her fierceness, her ability to get mad without seeming to fear a loss of love. The kinds of words that reverberated endlessly, impotently, inside Abby's head when she was angry with Michael poured forth from Sarah with no thought to anyone's feelings but her own. *I'M MAD AT YOU!* she would yell at times. *You're mean and I hate you! Don't ever look at me or talk to me ever, ever again!* And then, seconds later, it seemed, she might be smiling and filled with charm as she asked for a cookie, a story, a quick game of Candy Land, as though she had filled a bag with her anger and given it away, freeing herself as she burdened another.

Abby had said to her once, after Sarah had screamed at Stephanie that she would never ever play with her again, that it would be nice if they could apologize and be friends, and Sarah had looked at her mother with both sympathy and contempt. *But we* are *friends, Mom,* she said. *Don't you know that?*

Abby emerged from these thoughts as though from deep sleep and saw Miranda, looking directly into her eyes, a shy smile teasing her mouth. "It's like we're on an island here, you know? You and me? And all the problems feel far away."

"It feels safe," Abby said.

"It feels far away."

"Yeah."

There was a long silence before Miranda spoke again. "It was an island, too, at home with my father. He made it an island for me." She paused again. "I knew how to open the door."

Silence again, filling the room until it felt womblike. Miranda was fading away inside it, and to reach her, Abby asked, "Did you ever get lonely?"

Miranda flinched. Her eyes closed tight and then

opened again, her thumb brushed against her lips as though searching for an opening, a pathway to comfort.

"Sorry," Abby said, but it was too late. She watched as Miranda's thumb eased itself slowly, discreetly between her lips. *Ask the question of yourself,* Abby thought. *Are* you *lonely?* But it was not at all the same, of course. She had a husband, a son, a hospital, and a city full of friends. *Friends you don't see,* she told herself. *A husband and son who have wrapped their arms so tightly around each other that there is no longer room for you.*

Am I lonely? Abby asked herself again and knew even as she fought to push the knowledge away that the question contained its own answer. The flash of self-knowledge was painful, but feeling anything, even pain, seemed suddenly a comfort. In the silent room she became aware of noise. Cars rushed by outside; horns blared; dogs barked. Strange that she had not heard them before. She wondered, then, whether anyplace was truly silent. Even in the desert there must be wind, and the movement of sand upon sand.

She thought of the women that had made her dunes, people she truly loved. After Sarah died, she had let her pain erode their place in her life. Her sister . . . the summer after Sarah's death, Kate had dragged her to the Vineyard for a week, just the two of them, leaving the other survivors behind. On the first day, Kate had sat with her on the beach, watching the waves, while the air reverberated with the windblown sound of children playing and Abby longed to die. Kate was more careful after that, tending to Abby at home, buying lobster tails at twenty dollars a pound to go bad in the refrigerator, and talking in hushed tones when her children called to say good night. She had tried so hard to be a good sister; every hour, Abby had felt Kate's need for her to cry and cling so she could comfort her as a sister should. But Abby's eyes were dry as stones. *Well, I tried,* she could hear in her mind Kate saying after they got home. *You know how she gets. We all want to help, but she won't let anyone do a thing.* It was her fault yet again. She had seen little of Kate and her family after that.

Perhaps she should try to make new friends. She pictured herself at Ben's preschool, striking up a conversation, saying, *Hey, let's go grab a cup of coffee before work.* But who would she ask? Rebecca? Impossibly coiffed, perfectly made-up at eight thirty in the morning, and therefore out of the question. Denise? Agreeably rumpled but burdened with ten-month-old twins. Susan? Perky, chipper—annoyingly so. And the others, dropping off their kids in their suits and spotless sneakers, and hailing cabs for midtown offices, would have no time to chat even if Abby had found them worth her while. She had no time, either, of course. Between work and shopping and trying to spend time with Ben, there was no time at all for new relationships.

She missed her old friends, Melanie, Caroline. They had stormed the school together, linking arms and skipping through the corridors, singing at the top of their lungs, not caring. They had woven themselves together with threads of a million conversations replayed in smuggled notes and endless phone calls and code words whispered in the halls until their identities felt merged and safe. Until the boys came and the fabric began to tear: first Caroline, paired off with Steve, then Melanie, glued to James, and she was left standing alone. She remembered how lonely she had been then.

And I'm lonely now, she thought again, her voice a whine inside her mind. If she had been unaware of that ache before, now it seemed to fill her completely so that, as she sat with Miranda in the room, it seemed that she might fall inside it and disappear. She took a deep breath. It was almost the end of the session, anyway. When Miranda left, she would call Caroline. They had been friends since they were ten, after all, and if Abby had been a lousy friend since Sarah died, had refused a million offers and left as many phone calls unreturned, she knew that Carrie was not really angry, and would still be there to welcome her.

Having made a plan, Abby was astonished to feel a fierce, manic energy overwhelm her. The hunger, having lain dormant for so long, felt angry and insistent now that it had finally been acknowledged. Abby remembered reading about concentration camp survivors who recalled little hunger during captivity, but ate themselves into a gluttonous stupor upon their release. Her fingers stroked the phone on her desk, wove themselves into the cord. Yes. After Miranda left, she would call Caroline. She would make a date for lunch—no, screw that, for dinner—Michael could watch Ben, and Carrie's husband could babysit, too. She looked at the clock. Five minutes left in the session. What could she say, she wondered, to awaken this hunger in Miranda?

Softly, she said the girl's name, and Miranda raised her eyes. "Have you ever had a friend?" Abby asked.

"My father is my friend."

"No, I mean a friend your own age."

Miranda shook her head. "I will, though. When I am older. Daddy said he will find a friend for me to marry when I am older. Because you can never tell . . ."

"Never tell what?"

Silence.

"Never tell what, Miranda?" *And who said anything about marrying?*

Inside her mind, Miranda is listening to her father's voice. It thunders inside her head and hurts her ears. *Remember, girl,* he says. *You are a girl and you need to know this. The bad people in the world don't always dress in black. They don't have dirty teeth or stringy hair. They can be handsome on the outside, little girl. They can be golden-haired and dressed in silk, but the snakes will bite you just the same if you let them get too close.* Only her father could keep her safe. She knew that he was right, and she knew that when the time came, he would choose for her friends that would never hurt her, that would take care of her as her father did. But her mother (not-mother) must know this, too. Miranda feels briefly confused, and then relieved. Another test, one she knows she can pass.

"I know!" she said, triumphant. "*You* are my friend." And she looked up at Abby with joy and trust in her eyes.

Abby looked at her. "You're right. I am. Of course, I am." But that wasn't what she meant at all.

After Miranda left, Abby dialed Caroline's number from memory. *You have reached the office of Caroline Holland. I am either away from my desk or on another call. Please leave your name and number and I will return your call as soon as possible. Beep.*

Abby hesitated briefly, then spoke her name into the receiver, adding, "Remember me? I'm back from the dead. Give me a call when you can." Then she left her number and hung up.

Her fingers drummed the receiver. Who else was there? Melanie would be at work, too; an editor at a glossy magazine, she had often been available to schmooze in the middle of the day. Determined now, Abby thumbed through her address book until she found Melanie's number and then dialed it quickly, racing ahead of the voice in her mind telling her to just forget it. "Melanie Berman," she said when the receptionist answered.

"I'm sorry," said the disembodied voice. "She no longer works here. Would you like me to give you her new number?"

No longer works here? She and Melanie had been friends since junior high school. There was a time when Abby had known about each meal Melanie had, each pimple. Melanie's daughter, Rachel, had gone to preschool with Sarah; they had spent hours in the park, at the zoo, discussing toilet training, time-out strategies, how to stop the kids from burping at the table. And then she remembered, vaguely, as though it were a scene from a movie rather than from her own life, telling Melanie to stop calling, that hearing about Rachel was just too painful, and not hearing about her left a hole in the conversation that seemed to grow until it squeezed out thought. So Melanie had stopped. And Abby, somehow, had not even noticed. "Sure," she said, feeling suddenly tired. "I'll take the number."

She copied the numbers dutifully into her book, drawing a single line through the old information, and replaced the receiver in its cradle. It was as though by losing Sarah, she had lost a whole life.

Minutes later, when the phone rang, the sound was shrill, jarring. *Carrie*, thought Abby. *That was quick.* She picked up the receiver. "Hello?"

"Hi, Abby? It's Tom."

She felt her stomach swirl. "Hey, there," she said. "What's up?"

"I'm having a party at my house next weekend and I wondered if you wanted to come. You and Michael, of course," he added hastily.

The sudden racing of Abby's heart both embarrassed and amused her. "Well, thanks," she said. "We'd love to come."

Chapter Fifteen

Miranda finally understands. As she sits at her desk in the row of desks and stares at the dark brown hair that blankets the boy's head in front of her, it comes to her, the bone truth that sends a jolt throughout her body like fire racing across a plain. When he turns and looks at her, wetting his lips like a cat with his moist red tongue, and does not break his gaze until she looks away, she knows again that she is right.

His name is Freddy. She watches him with the no-more-dead-beaver girl, Natalie. She sees him come to Natalie and rub up against her and retreat, like a wave crashing on a beach, and Miranda wonders, sometimes, how it would feel to be the sand he crashes against. He sits in front of her in the class, but when they pull their chairs into a circle in the dayroom, he always pulls his own chair next to hers.

They sit next to each other, and she feels the heat from his body wrap itself around her and draw her in, holding tighter and tighter until she cannot move. She does not want to move. And she understands, because her father has warned her about the snakes so many times, that this boy has a power that can kill. She wants to be killed, because this is what she now understands. It is a knowledge so simple that she wants to laugh because she has not seen it before: if she is bitten by the snake, then she, Miranda, will die *and be reborn,* not as herself, a frail fleshy girl, but as a boy, as straight and hard as the boy who sits before her and next to her and wills himself into her despite all the warnings, despite her father, despite herself. She wants to welcome the snake with open arms.

Her father wants a boy; she has always known that. *I wish you had been a boy, Miranda. There is nothing out there that can hurt a boy.* If she were a boy, her father would not have to be afraid for her, would not have to keep her locked up safe against the dangers of the world. If she were a boy, she could be free.

She is playing checkers with Natalie. Freddy stands behind them, watching.

"Winners," he says.

Miranda skates her pieces across the red-and-black sea, jumping them over the waves like the bonny boat in the song her father used to sing:

> *Speed, bonny boat, like a bird on the wing,*
> *Onward the sailors cry.*
> *Carry the lad, that is born to be king,*
> *Over the sea, to Skye.*

She loved that song, loved the rich deep voice that sang it, and now she knows, as the song plays over and over in her mind, that her father was telling her even then: *she was the bonny boat, and inside her lived that lad that was born to be king.*

Her piece has reached the other side in safety. "King me," she says, and Natalie puts another checker on top of the first.

"Go, girl!" Freddy says, and reaches out to slap her hand.

The slap stings like a snakebite and Miranda feels herself recoil. Inside herself, she checks for signs of change and, disappointed, finds none. Only a whisper of fear. Her hand reaches out to guide her pieces, lifting them over the other girl's. *Jump, jump, jump.*

Freddy's laugh is harsh. "Shit, Nat. You suck. Know that? You really suck."

"Shut up, asshole."

Frightened, Miranda looks up, but Natalie is smiling. They speak in code, and she knows that she does not really understand.

"Come on, *Randy,*" says the boy. "Your turn."

Miranda looks down at the board and sees only two black circles swimming like sharks in the sea. Her king can conquer them with ease. *Jump, jump,* and the circles are gone.

"Yo, Randy! Randy rules—Natsie drools!"

"Oh, fuck you," Natalie says, but her voice is soft like buttered bread and she slides her heavy body out of her chair without knocking over the board. Grandly, she gestures at the chair. "See if *you* can beat her, turd breath, before you go mocking me."

Miranda looks at the boy sitting in front of her. His white shirt is tight over his rippled skin, showing bulges that are wide and hard like armor across his chest. She wonders how it would feel to hold her head against them as she sometimes does against her father's chest, to have the boy's strong arms around her, protecting her, as her father's arms have done when she has felt frightened or alone.

"Are we going to play, or what?"

Miranda sucks in her breath and looks down. "Sorry."

They set up their pieces and take turns sliding them back and forth, jumping and eluding, until Freddy has three kings and two other pieces, and Miranda two kings standing alone. Watching her boats in the sea, sliding and sinking, Miranda hears the voices of the children from far away, like laughter from the street on a summer night. She follows the boy's hands moving in and out as he guides his circles along the black paths, sees that the fingers are squat and strong and covered with hair. He brushes them against her as he reaches for his checker and this time they do not bite.

"Let's make it interesting," he says. "If you win, I'll give you a dollar, okay?"

Natalie makes a sound like a pig. "Yeah? And if you win? She ain't got no money. What the fuck she gonna give you?"

"A fuck," he says.

"Yeah, right. Don't listen to him, Miri. He be shittin' you."

"No, I'm kidding. You don't have to give me no fuck, Randy. Just a kiss, okay? You win, I give you a dollar. I win, you give me a kiss. Whaddya say?"

Miranda imagines his lips on hers, feels herself absorbed within him, melting but at the same time gaining strength. She does not feel afraid. "Yes," her voice answers, and she nods her head twice.

"Awesome!"

"You don't know what you doin', girl." Natalie is shaking her head, but the dead beaver is gone and Natalie is laughing and light and Miranda feels that Natalie is wrong, and that for the first time, she knows exactly what she does.

Two minutes later, Miranda's pieces are gone and the board is awash in black. Freddy rubs his hands together. "That's it. I win. Time to pay up."

She sees his face approach her like a spaceship, his eyes as bright as searchlights, blinding her as they move closer and closer until they fill her vision, until all she can see is him. She feels his lips press warm and hard against hers, and then she is gone.

Later, alone in her room, she returns to feel the simmering heat. The noises of the summer, horns, dogs, bursts of laughter, salsa music, and gangsta rap, seem to seep into the humid air and travel through the grated gray windows. There will be time, her father says, and there is time. But in this time Miranda sees no stitches. Instead, the minutes seem strewn across space, like beads let loose from a broken necklace. She lies on her back and lets her hand slide down her belly, then down still more, under the elastic of her underpants to feel if her penis has begun to grow. She feels nothing but the smallest bump, and as she rubs her hand against the bump a space of pure feeling opens like a balloon inside her. Faster

and faster she rubs as the balloon grows bigger and then finally pops, and she drifts down gently into sleep.

When she wakes, her father is there. She sits, and he
cradles her head against his chest.

"Miri, Miri," she hears, and the voice comes through his
chest and into her ear and curls against her like a cat until she
feels safe. "I will take you away." He sits on her bed with her
and it is warm and still, and in the long, deep quiet comes her
father's voice again, where it echoes as in a tunnel: "I will
never forgive them for what they've done to you."

In a flash of light Miranda sees Freddy, Natalie, Abby
Cohen, too, their hair a wreath of flames that gives warmth
but does not burn. They have done nothing; there is nothing to forgive. She knows what he sees—the dirty
bathrobes, the sagging couches stained with piss, the ragged
half-clad children in slippers and blue pajamas—but she has
no words to tell him what it is to her. In her mind there are
pictures: yellow eggs and brown toast on a plastic plate, the
line of sun sweeping over the checkered linoleum, the for-
est of hair on Freddy's arms, and the full red roundness of
his lips. Though the world seems jagged here, the edges are
soft. There are people but no snakes. Nothing to be afraid
of, after all. She pulls away and looks up at him. "Do you
know how to play checkers?"

"Checkers?"

"Yes. Natalie taught me. I like it. Do you?"

Jack smiled, but he was not happy. She had surprised
him, this girl-child, and he did not like surprises. He felt
trapped. "Checkers, huh?"

"Yes. Can we play?" She pauses and looks at his face, but

she cannot tell what he thinks. Her father loves her. He wants her to be happy. "I like it," she repeats so that he will be sure.

Checkers. Jack snorted softly and wondered what else they had taught her. She was a genie, let out of the bottle, and as he thought this he saw in his mind that genie on TV, *I Dream of Jeannie,* all breasts and curves and undulating scarves, and he heard his own mother's voice in his mind: *A little knowledge is a dangerous thing.* Once the genie was out of the bottle, it was not so easy to put it back in. He looked down at her face and saw wanting, eagerness. He wanted to slap her. "I don't know how to play," he snapped.

Miranda takes the blow. "I thought—"

"Maybe I knew once, all right? But I've forgotten. It's a stupid game. Stupid. A waste of time." He breathed—in, out, in, out—and willed his voice to calm. "Have you even done your homework?"

Miranda is silent, feeling the burn of his words.

"Well? They've got you in school, right? Aren't they giving you homework?"

She nods her head yes, rubbing her ear against his chest before he pushes her head roughly away.

"And?" Jack said. "Have you done it?"

Miranda tenses, waiting for the fear she knows will come, but feels only the steady burning of a small bright flame. "No," she says, and her eyes look straight at his.

"Well, do it. Now. It's almost dinnertime. What are you doing lazing in bed, anyway? Are you a cow? Huh? That's what cows do, you know. Sleep away the day chewing on their cud. Is that what they've got you doing now? Huh? Is that what it is?"

She looks at him and sees his nose growing big and red on his face and his mouth flap-flap-flapping like a clown's. Her lips curl up and then his hand is on her wrist, squeezing like a snake, biting into her flesh. "Don't laugh at me, girl."

She tries to pull her arm away, but his grip is too strong. "You're hurting me!"

"Good," he said, but he loosened his grip and her arm dropped to the bed. His heart was pounding so hard that he could hear the blood pulsing in his ears. Looking up, he saw the metal mesh on the windows, the dirty smudges on the walls. It was filthy here, filthy. He needed to get out. "I'm leaving," he told his daughter, "but I'll be back. And I want that work done."

When she spoke, her voice was loud and strong. "And then can we play? I can teach you. It's easy."

"We'll see," Jack said sharply. He left, pounding powerfully down the hall toward the elevators. And saw that bitch, that Cohen, walking toward him.

"Is everything all right?" she asked, that phony shrink concern dripping like maple syrup from her mouth.

"Your days are numbered, Doc," he said, without ever breaking stride.

When her father leaves, Miranda's room implodes into darkness. In darkness, she goes to her backpack and retrieves her school folder, laying it open on her bed. More math that they've given her, but the numbers are dull, inert on the page. She stares at them until her hand begins to move, guiding the pencil across the page, slowly at first and then faster and faster, harder and harder, bearing down until the page is dark and filled with holes. And finally, when the numbers are gone and the page lies shredded on the bed, Miranda lies still.

Abby stood in the doorway, watching Miranda. "Hi," she said, and noted the fierceness and fear commingled on the face that looked up from the bed. "I saw your father in the hallway a minute ago." Abby paused, unsure how much to reveal. "He seemed . . ."

Miranda scooped up the shreds of blackened paper, crushing them in her hands. "I don't care." Her voice was low, directed to the bed rather than to Abby.

"Kind of mad," Abby finished. "Did something happen?"

Outside, the sun burned bright and hot behind the dirty window. Her father was mad, but it did not rain. "The king is dead," Miranda said. "Long live the king."

"I'm sorry?" Abby walked to the bed and sat down next to the girl.

"My father told me," Miranda said. "You know, in England. Like there had to be a king all the time, every second, to protect the people, and so when the king would die that's what they'd say. The king is dead. The king is dead. Long live the king."

It was, Abby thought, the longest flow of words Miranda had ever given her. And she had no idea what the girl was trying to say. "And so did someone just die? A king?"

Miranda looked at her with pity. "It isn't raining."

Obligingly, Abby looked out the window. "Nope. It's a beautiful day."

"So you see."

No, kid, Abby thought, *I'm afraid I don't.* "Can you tell me more?"

Miranda was silent for a long time before she finally answered. "There is nothing more to tell."

Chapter Sixteen

When the evening of the party finally came, Abby made her way to Tom's building and then stood before the door of his apartment, listening to the music and laughter inside, deciding whether to ring the bell. Her stomach felt loose and her skin was cool and moist. She reached forward to press the buzzer and then let her hand drop to her side. In the dim hallway light she saw five other doors and wondered briefly about the lives being lived inside. A dog's bark echoed down the stairwell, deep and rough, and a man's voice said, "Shhhhhhh." Her hands remembered stroking fur, scratching ears, how good it felt. Maybe they should get a dog. She would have to talk to Michael.

Behind her, the elevator stopped and she heard the door open. She recognized Judy, a paralegal in Tom's department, and a tall, thin young man who must have been her date. "Abby! Hi! Are you coming or going?"

"Just got here."

"Well, were you planning to go in?"

"Of course! I was just cooling off a minute, catching my breath. I guess I should have taken the bus, but I waited forever, so—"

"Probably cooler inside."

"Right." She rang the bell and there was a brief pause before she heard footsteps approach and Tom opened the door. The foyer was bright, welcoming, with hardwood floors and a collection of animal masks, too colorful to be African—Australian, perhaps? or South American?—hanging on the walls. He had put on a CD, rather too loud, Abby thought, and the notes of a flute and a jazz piano filled the air.

"Well, hi," Tom said, kissing Abby and Judy on the cheek and shaking hands with Judy's friend as he ushered them in, directing them to drinks and food. When Judy had gone, Tom turned to Abby. "I was beginning to think you might not make it."

"I almost didn't. The babysitter canceled at the last minute, and Michael couldn't get home before eight."

"The phantom Michael. Does he really exist, or is he just a figment of your twisted mind?"

"Right. I made him up, actually, to keep my legions of admirers at bay."

"Aha! Just as I suspected."

The doorbell rang again and Tom went to answer it as Abby wandered into the party. She poured a glass of wine and took it down two steps into a sunken living room, winding with manufactured purpose around groups of people she did not know, engaged in conversations she did not have the energy to enter. A baby grand piano, with a

Rodgers and Hart songbook open on the music stand, stood incongruously in the corner, filling a quarter of the room. Abby ran her finger lightly over the keys, making a soft, muffled series of notes, as she looked at a row of pictures in silver frames that stood up against the piano's black lacquer finish. Among the shots of handsome brown-haired children and handsome white-haired adults, she recognized in one a youngish Tom with shoulder-length hair and a bandanna tied around his head, sitting on the top of a mountain with his arm around a girl, their flushed faces framed against a Kodachrome blue sky. She picked it up and held it close to her face, studying it as though she might be asked to remember a detail later on.

"And she wonders, old girlfriend? Ex-wife?" Tom's voice startled her and she put the picture down quickly, feeling that she had been caught unguarded in a secret, shameful act.

"I was looking at you, actually. Nice hair."

"Thanks. And it's my sister." He pointed to the pictures of the children. "These are her kids, my niece and nephew. Just in case you were wondering."

Abby gestured to the piano. "So you play?"

"No. But I needed a place to put my photos, and a bookshelf seemed so conventional."

"Funny."

The noises of the party swelled around them. Tom left her side to refill the ice bucket, and all around her people formed clusters and then broke away to join others, like a collection of molecules bouncing through space. Conversations ebbed and flowed in rhythmic tides and the room grew warm despite the frantic workings of the air conditioner. As she drank her second glass of wine, the party began to seem like fun.

"So did you hear about our new admit today? Tyrell?" Steve Blauner, the psychiatrist on the adult acute-psychosis unit, had joined Abby in the corner. She shook her head. "Well, he's putting on quite a show, screaming and spitting and kicking. The guy must weigh, like, three hundred pounds, and we're getting out the Haldol and restraints, the whole nine yards, when all of a sudden he goes dead still and quiet, and we all stand there, frozen, waiting to see what he's going to do."

"And?"

"And then all of a sudden he goes, 'Shit, man, where are we? You got some great music! Are we in a disco? Is this a disco?' "

Abby laughed.

"So then Roger's standing right there. You know, Mr. Seventies throwback? And right on cue he starts to sing that Talking Heads song, you know, 'This ain't no party! This ain't no disco!' " Steve was laughing and Abby joined in. "We're making it our theme song."

"You guys have all the fun."

"It's been wild, I tell you. And what's new on Tower Ten?"

Miranda, Abby thought, but she did not want to turn her into a story. So instead she told about a new kid, Danny, who had been caught the week before trying to elope in his hospital pajamas and slippers. Which wouldn't have been so funny, except that he got all the way to Brooklyn on the D train before he was stopped.

"The D train, huh?" Steve said. "Well, no wonder. He probably blended right in."

"The funny thing is, he seems calmer now that he's back. Like he's happy to be home." When Steve left to refill his drink, Abby wandered to the window and watched the cars stampede like manic animals down Columbus Avenue, their headlights glowing like eyes, lighting up the night. This was her city, after all; she took comfort in the endless parade of people that she did not know passing by as though they were characters in a book she might someday get to read. She remembered a friend of hers, Jackie, who had moved to Dallas after college, complaining that the people one did not talk to in Texas seemed so much less interesting than those one did not talk to in New York. Apartment lights glowed warm and welcoming across the street. She watched a man in a T-shirt settle in a chair as a television flickered in the corner. From across Columbus Avenue she could tell that he, like Michael at home, was watching baseball. On the floor above, a couple embraced, their bodies pressed so close together that they might have been a statue, carved out of a single block of stone. Then the man reached up and the room went dark.

As a child, Abby had once stood before a window like this, in her parents' apartment on the thirteenth floor, and thought for long minutes about what it would be like to jump. She remembered the cool press of glass against her forehead as she had looked down at the street below, imagining the sudden absence of fear and pain and sound, only the wind rushing by as the pavement rose to meet her. How sad her parents would be, she had thought.

In the air outside, Abby smelled hot Szechuan oil and pizza dough. She remembered that she had not eaten, and thought, rather than felt, that she must be hungry. It was night now; the long summer twilight had finally faded to black, but there were no stars. All the lights of the world seemed to shimmer below her, as though she were God looking down on creation. But she did not believe in God.

"Having a good time?" Tom was standing at her elbow, offering a bite-sized piece of rice, crab, and avocado wrapped invitingly in smooth green seaweed.

"Mmmmm, thanks." Abby took a bite. "I am, actually," she said as she chewed.

"Are you always this much fun at parties?"

"Just about."

"Oh, well. Forewarned is forearmed, I guess." He lapsed into silence beside her.

"So," Abby asked as the silence grew stiff, "I missed Grand Rounds this week. Anything earth-shattering go on?"

"She makes conversation!"

Abby blushed. "Am I that hard to talk to?"

"Not at all. I could talk to you for hours. The question is, would you ever say anything back?"

"Occupational hazard. I get paid to listen, you know."

"Consider yourself officially off the job."

"All right. What would you like to talk about?"

"You," he said. "Tell me about you."

I had a daughter who died, Abby thought. *That's all there is to tell.* She did not want to talk about Sarah, not here in the noisy living room. How gauche it would be, bringing tragedy to a party, spoiling everyone's good time. But the fact of Sarah's death sat like a lump of undigested food at the back of Abby's throat, blocking words. She could talk about Michael and Ben, bringing them to the party, but they were a part of her that Tom would not want to share. "I grew up around here, you know. On Eighty-fifth Street. We could have been neighbors."

"Except that I lived in Kansas."

"Kansas!"

"No *Wizard of Oz* jokes, please." He was smiling, and Abby saw a tiny sliver of seaweed stuck between his teeth. "We can't all be urban sophisticates like you."

"How long have you lived in the city?"

"Oh, about seven years now. I moved here for law school, and then—" He shrugged.

"You got sucked in, like all the rest."

"I like it now. But it took me years to stop missing the sky."

She felt the loneliness in his words echo inside herself. "You never stop missing it, really."

"The sky?" Tom asked, but Abby was thinking how the missing itself was like a sky, a vast, empty expanse opening up inside her, filling and stretching her until her skin was thin as paper and she felt that she might float away. She had not been to many parties since Sarah had died; she shouldn't have come tonight.

From across the room, a couple called their thanks to Tom and he left to say good-bye. As though the moon had waned, the tide of people in the room began to ebb back into the night, grabbing bags and kissing one another, thanking Tom for the food and the evening, and yelling ahead to please hold the elevator. Gratefully, Abby joined them.

"Sorry we didn't really get to talk," Tom said as she left.

"Another time, perhaps."

"Promise?"

"Sure."

Outside, the air had grown cooler. She began walking up Columbus Avenue, past sidewalk cafés with laughing, chewing people, with men in torn jeans and Nike sneakers holding cups of coins out to them as they ate. The people walking past her all seemed to be in pairs, like a parade of animals lining up to board the ark. On every corner, bins of fruit, purple and red and green, lay beckoning. A pound of plums, Abby noted, cost two forty-nine, but she bought one anyway, biting into the gently yielding flesh as she walked. At Eighty-ninth Street, she turned left toward Amsterdam, moving unafraid through the empty darkness toward the rich smell of horses housed in the Claremont Stables at the end of the block. She had learned to ride in those rings, learned to love the feeling of the horses' strong flanks underneath her calves and the rub of leather against her thighs as she trotted in figure eights across the sawdust. She had favored a scrawny roan mare, as awkward and ungainly as she had felt herself to be. Somehow in each other they had each found grace. They had been fused, in Abby's mind at least, into one, a centaur, cantering like rolling water as the teacher flicked her crop. She remembered her mother, standing in her skirt and starched shirt and pumps with the other parents outside the ring and looking up from a conversation to follow the horse and rider with her eyes for what seemed a long, long time before she looked away. Abby heard a horse's whinny in the dark and shivered, suddenly cold.

She had left her jacket at Tom's.

She could call when she got home, ask him to bring it into work on Monday. But she might need it over the weekend. And she was cold now.

She turned and began walking back the way she had come. *There is no such thing as an accident,* she thought. Basic Freud—she had not even had to wait for graduate school to learn that. It was not true, of course. People had accidents all the time. They tripped and fell over uneven pavement, swerved cars around deer and crashed into trees, dropped hot cups of coffee into their laps. Freud had meant something different. He had meant that leaving your jacket in the apartment of a man you had flirted with for most of the evening and half the previous week so that you had to go back to the apartment instead of going home to your emotionally estranged husband and sleeping son was probably motivated by an unconscious wish of some undetermined type and was thus probably not "an accident." That was what he had meant.

From outside the door, Abby could hear a piano. She rang the bell and the music stopped. "Who is it?"

"It's Abby." She heard the sound of locks clicking open, and then he was standing there, smiling. Behind him, she could see her jacket, neatly folded and hung over the back of a chair.

"You forgot your jacket."

"How'd you guess?"

"I was wondering whose it was. I would have brought it to work, you know, if you'd called."

Abby looked at him. "I know."

"Do you want to come in?"

"For a minute. Could I use your bathroom?"

"You have fifty cents?"

"You're hilarious."

"I know. I got a million of them."

From the bathroom, she heard the music start again, a tune that sounded familiar and sweet. She dried her hands and stood at the top of the stairs for a moment, listening, before going down to stand beside him. "What are you playing?"

"Rodgers and Hart," he said. " 'I Could Write a Book.' Sit down, if you want, and I'll play it for you. It's a great song."

She settled awkwardly onto the couch, embarrassed by the idea of a serenade. "No one's ever sung to me before. Are you sure you don't have a balcony or a parapet I could lean on?"

"Shut up and listen, before I lose my nerve." And then he sang, in a voice surprisingly rich and deep:

> *If they asked me, I could write a book*
> *About the way you walk and whisper and*
> *look.*
> *I could write a preface on how we met*
> *So the world would never forget.*

She had heard the song before, she remembered, on an old Ella Fitzgerald record her father used to play.

"'You're right," Abby said. "I love this song."

Tom stopped playing. "Me, too. I've been playing it a lot lately. Thinking of you."

Abby could feel her face grow warm. "Tom—"

"Do you want to hear the rest of the song?"

"Sure."

> *And the simple secret of the plot*
> *Is just to tell them that I love you a lot;*
> *And the world discovers, as my book*
> *ends*
> *How to make two lovers of friends.*

And then he was moving toward her, as slow and steady as a shark. *He is going to kiss me,* she thought, and felt a warmth spread down her throat and into her stomach as though she had drunk cocoa, hot and sweet. "Abby," he said, and space and time seemed suddenly limitless and she herself alive. A rush of heat moved upward through her skin until she felt the lightest touch might sear her flesh. It was this that she had wanted after all: not the kiss itself, but this moment that hung before it filled with hope, like the rush of cool breeze before a rain.

When he kissed her at last, his lips felt dry and slightly chapped. He pushed his tongue inside her mouth, hungry and insistent, but for her the moment was gone. There was Michael to think of, and Ben, and Sarah, too, and the knowledge in her body sure and deep that this was not what she wanted, after all. She pulled away. "I don't think I can do this."

"Why not? Michael?" Tom's tone was wheedling. "You know he's just a figment."

"It's not just that." She struggled to sit up and pulled her legs under her, facing him on the couch. Her heart was pounding, the blood pulsing in her ears with each beat, her stomach contracting and releasing as though she were giving birth to a pounding ocean. *Breathe,* the nurse had told her when Sarah was born. *Get on top of it,* she'd said. *Get on top of this, lady,* Abby had said. She remembered the animal terror of being torn apart from inside that she had felt in that bed, when her body with its raging need to push had subsumed thought and brought screaming, searing pain and then, like a gift after anger, delivered to her the crowning soft jet-black head of her baby and pure joy.

"What?" Tom said. "What is it?"

She took a deep breath. "I had a daughter. And she died."

He inhaled sharply and recoiled, like a swimmer sticking a toe into icy water, and then he leaned toward her and took her hand. "Tell me," he said. And she began to speak.

Chapter Seventeen

Not every day but some days her mother (not-mother) comes to her. She says her name and takes her into the room with flowers and a shelf of animals made of glass. At first the room was filled with silence, but more and more now there are words and sounds that might even be crying. There is sun in the room that slants through blinds and falls in lines across the floor, and tiny specks of dust that dance in the light like miniature angels. She is careful not to ever breathe them in.

It is cool in the room and Miranda pulls her sweater close around her shoulders. The woman notices and says *Would you like me to turn the air conditioner down?* but Miranda does not answer because she is thinking of something else. "You asked me if I remember, and I don't. But my body does. My body remembers things."

"What?" her mother asks. "What does your body remember?"

"It remembers the wind."

"The wind?"

"I can feel it on my arms and face sometimes, like breath, even when the windows are closed."

"Breath?"

"And swinging. In my stomach. Up and down, out and in with my legs. It feels like flying. And like coming back. I'm tethered, like a falcon. Do you know about falcons?"

Abby shakes her head no, but Miranda goes on without waiting for an answer. "They belonged to kings. The kings would bind their legs with lines and then pretend to let them fly free, to hunt, I think, or fight, if the kings wanted them to, but all along the kings would hold the string. Do you see? They could never fly farther than the kings would let them."

It is quiet in the room, and in her mind Miranda watches as a bird with chestnut feathers that drip from its wings like hair sits on a swing and then turns into a girl who pumped strong legs up into the sky and leaned back to see a woman's upside-down smile recede and return and recede again as her back felt the press of hands sending her giddy and unafraid into the air again. There are other things her body remembers: the twining of hands and the press of a ring against her finger, sweat-slick in the summer heat; the smell of perfume on her mother's neck; the brush of lips against her cheek. She sees her in her mind, her real mother, with curly black hair flecked with strands of iron gray, and skin freckled from the sun, and eyes as green as grass that told Miranda without words that she was good and she was loved.

When she looks up again, she sees a woman who is not her mother and not a god and has no fire in her hair but sits quietly watching with that same look in her eyes. Her body feels raw, burning, like a frozen hand plunged into warm water.

"What do you think about the falcons?" Abby asked gently. "Do you think they wanted to be free?"

"I think they were scared."

"Scared?"

"It's funny, you know? I think they would have stayed with the kings anyway, even if they hadn't been tethered. They were fed, right? And safe? But the kings didn't know."

"And if they had known?" Abby asked. "Do you think they would have set them free?"

Miranda became so still that Abby was not sure she would speak. Their session was almost over, and she was about to tell Miranda that she would see her on Thursday, when the girl gave her answer. "No. I don't. The kings would never have trusted their birds, I think. They were only birds. The kings would never have been sure of their love." She paused. "They were sad, those kings. Don't you think?"

"They must have loved those birds."

Miranda nodded. "I think they did."

"And those memories in your body," Abby said. "Your body is *you*, Miranda. The memories are yours; *you* remember. And maybe, next time, you'll remember some more, and we can talk about that, too."

That was the end; it was time to go. As they left the room together, Miranda gave her hand to Abby, and let the tall, thin woman lead her down the hall.

★ ★ ★

My body remembers things. . . . Abby heard the words in her mind for days as she felt her own body stir with memories that seemed to exist not in her mind but in the cells of her flesh. Walking down the street, she might feel the sweaty fullness of a child's hand nestled in her own, or the ticklish, sensual warmth of a child's secret being whispered in her ear. As the memories returned, her body felt denser, more substantial. It was as though she had been merely an outline of a person in a child's coloring book and had emerged, fully hued, into a three-dimensional world.

She had not seen Tom since the party. The tears she had shed as she sat in his embrace and talked about her daughter, like a thundershower on a hot August day, had washed away desire, leaving only warmth. She had disgorged the flood of memory that had filled her; she was raw and empty, yearning, wanting not Tom but Michael and Ben and the life that had seethed all along, underneath her pain.

She wanted to go home.

Ben sensed the change immediately. It frightened him, the voracious, guilty love of this new mother, and he responded by becoming clingy and demanding. He needed her every few minutes, it seemed. For days, the house rang with his whiny voice calling her to his side. *Mommy, I need help with the toilet paper! Mommy, I can't find my truck! Mommy, I need some more juice! Mommy, I need you to come right now!* One morning, she determined to count how many times he said *Mommy* during a day, but by ten o'clock the count was over one hundred, and she simply gave up. It was as though he sensed her awakening, and wanted to be sure he would be noticed when at last her eyes were opened.

But when she gave him the attention he craved, he turned willful, testing every limit she set for him. One night, when Michael was working late and she was eating dinner alone with Ben, at last ready to focus on him, he refused to even look at her. Instead, he narrowed his gaze to his new toy car, *vroom*ing it along the table and around his plate.

"No toys at the table, honey," Abby said.

He ignored her.

"Benjamin."

Silence.

"Do I need to take it away from you?"

He increased the car's velocity and, as she reached to take it from him, slammed it into his cup, splashing milk all over himself. Panicked, he jumped up and began to cry.

"Benjamin!" she yelled. "How many times have I told you that we don't play with toys at the table? Now do you see what happens? Look at this mess!" She grabbed a wad of paper towels and started toward him as he hopped up and down near his chair.

"Ahhhh! I'm wet! Mommy! Take my shirt off! It feels yucky!"

"That's what you get," she said. But as she pulled his soggy shirt over his head and met his gaze, she saw the fear in his eyes. She had never meant to frighten him.

"I'm sorry," he pleaded. "It was an accident. Are you mad at me?" Suddenly, Abby felt herself looking not sideways but with full force at the half-naked child before her. Sarah's ghost was gone. She felt her throat grow tight with love and she gathered his body to her and rocked him in her arms, her child, her little boy.

He wriggled out of her grasp. "Are you, Mom?"

Abby swallowed hard, fighting tears. "I think we need a bubble bath, bubba," she said, making Ben giggle in spite of himself. She clutched at him. "I love you, Benjo," she said, suddenly desperate for him to feel it. She had given him so little, after all.

"I love you, too." He let her hold him for a moment, before he wriggled free and galloped ahead of her, down the hall.

By the time Michael came home, Ben had been successfully bathed and was cuddled in bed, listening to her read a story. He barely looked at his father, smiling in the doorway, before he urged her to keep reading.

"This is a cozy scene," Michael said.

Abby smiled. "There's leftover pizza for dinner, if you're hungry."

"Sounds delicious."

"Homemade, I mean."

"Yum."

"Mom! Stop talking to Daddy and finish my story."

"Sorry, sweetie." She cuddled him close and began to read, watching Michael from the corner of her eye as he stood watching them. She knew him so well, had seen so many times that loving look that held along with affection and pleasure a smug sort of paternal pride. Watching him watch her, she felt herself begin to act a part, good mother, good wife—drop in the quarter, folks, wind her up, and see how well she performs. And she thought, for the first time, that maybe he was playing a part, too. Good husband, good father. How long had it been since she had really looked at him? Seeing him now, standing in the doorway, reaching up to loosen his tie, she realized that he looked old. The lines around his mouth had deepened, and his neck had grown slack and full, spilling over his buttoned collar. Her mouth continued to say the words of the story, rhythmic rhymes about Horton the faithful elephant who sat through danger and loneliness on someone else's egg until it hatched into a baby that cleaved to him, forsaking the mother who had abandoned him. *And it should be*, she read, *it should be, it should be like that. Because Horton was faithful, he sat and he sat.* Looking at Michael as she read those words, she felt a rush of gratitude that made her want to gather him, too, in her arms, and rock him as she had rocked her son.

But they were adults and it was not so simple. Alone with Michael after Ben was finally asleep, she felt almost shy. "So how was your day?" she asked. "Anything interesting?"

He shrugged, eyes not moving from the TV screen. "Not really. Just the usual."

And you? she asked herself in her mind. *How was your day, hon?* But he was silent. She swallowed her irritation and tried again. "Did you finish the paper you were working on?"

"Almost."

"Michael—"

He looked up, annoyed. "What?"

I kissed another man, she thought. *But I think that I wanted to be kissing you.* "Nothing. I love you."

He smiled and looked back at the TV. "That's nice, sweetie. I love you, too."

But that wasn't what I meant, she thought. *That wasn't it at all*. And how foolish of her, to expect him to sense this change in her, or trust it, or match his mood to hers. She remembered how they used to shift their bodies in tandem through the night as they slept together in the dorm-issued single bed. They had not been that close in years.

The dryer buzzed in the kitchen, and Abby tumbled the warm clothes out into the laundry basket. She pressed one of Michael's shirts against her face, breathing in the scent of detergent and fabric softener that had erased all traces of her husband's smell. One by one she folded the clothes, piling them on top of the dryer in three separate stacks. Ben was big enough to wear Sarah's old clothes now, Abby thought. She should really take them out of their box in the back of the closet. But of course she never would. And soon Ben would be too big for them, would be bigger and older than Sarah would ever grow, would be a teenager, would leave for college, would get married and move away, and then Michael would leave, too, because her gravity would not be enough to hold him, and he would spin away from her out into space.

Standing there, in the warmth of the kitchen, Michael's half-folded shirt in her hand, she suddenly understood that in some deep and poorly grasped part of herself, she had already said good-bye. She would never let herself be caught unaware again, as she had when Sarah got sick.

She thought of Miranda, cloistered in her father's house like Rapunzel in her tower, safe from love and loss. Since Sarah's death, she, too, had been imprisoned. For two years she had watched as Michael circled her fortress, lacking courage, lacking will, a most dispirited knight, as much in need of rescue as she. She thought of Tom, too, but knew that while he might join her in her tower, even bring some joy to her there, she could never really love him; he could never set her free. She imagined herself walking in to Michael now, confessing her transgression. Impossible.

Instead, she hoisted the laundry basket and carried it back to their room. Words fluttered like birds through her mind. *You seem so far away,* she might begin. *Michael, I miss you.* She picked up the remote and turned off the television.

"Hey," he protested. "I was watching that."

"I know." Her hands trembled as she laid the clothes on his dresser and smoothed the still-warm cloth. Nervously, she rubbed her dry lips together and struck what she hoped was a seductive pose. "I thought I'd go to bed soon. Any interest in joining me?"

His eyes scanned her face, then looked away. "I'd love to, but . . . it's early, and I've still got some work I need to do. Maybe later, all right?"

"Can I try to persuade you?"

"Really, no." She sighed, and he sat up. She had annoyed him. "For Christ's sake, Ab—I can wait for weeks while *you're too tired,* but you act wounded when I don't snap to attention the minute you want me to."

"It's not that. It's just—sometimes you seem so far away."

"So?" He paused, as though deciding whether to continue.

"What?"

"Never mind."

"No," she insisted. "Tell me what you were going to say."

He shrugged, as though speaking to her required an energy that he no longer possessed. "It's just . . . you know, you've pushed and pushed and pushed me away until I feel like I'm as dead to you as she is. So now, all right, I'm far away." He picked up a pencil from the night table and rolled it in his hand. "I'm far away," he repeated. "Isn't that where you wanted me to be?"

"Maybe. Maybe I did." She ran her hands through her hair. There was so much she wanted to say, but the silence between them muffled her thoughts. With an effort, she spoke again. "But now I want to be close."

"Fine," he retorted. "Just draw me a map, okay? Mark my spot with an *X*."

They paused, each breathing hard. When Abby spoke again, her voice was soft. "I wasn't the only one pushing, you know."

"I know." He reached out to pull her next to him on the bed. She felt her eyes blur with tears at this unexpected gesture, and she rested her head on his chest, listening to his heartbeat. "Really, I know. I'm sorry."

"Me, too." Eyes closed, she thought of a night long ago when she had walked with him through the snow by the frozen Charles River. It had been their third or fourth date, when they were just getting to be friends and were not yet lovers. They had come warm and smiling out of a movie theater, into the winter night, and the feeling had been like biting into something both spicy and delicious. It had been snowing all day and the ground was covered with a thick white quilt. She had turned to him as they walked along, her breath forming fog in the air, and asked whether he would mind if she pushed him down into the snow. *No,* he had said, and in that instant she had come at him with all her weight, catching him off-balance, although, as she said later many times, he had been warned, and pushing him backward into a drift. She had fallen on top of him then, feeling the warmth of his breath and the cold of his cheek as he drew her close and kissed her; she'd seen the snowflakes in his eyelashes sparkling like stars, smelled the pine smoke blowing down from the chimneys, and tasted him as his tongue danced with hers.

I can't believe you did that, he had said.

And she had laughed, feeling a child's pleasure in surprise. It was no longer so easy to catch him off guard.

"What are you thinking about?" he asked.

"Just you," she said.

"Oh, that."

His heart beat in her ear, steady and safe. The sound lulled her into a state akin to calm, and when she spoke again it was as though the words were spoken in a dream. "Do you remember that time she and Steffi played at our house, and they glued their hands together so Steffi wouldn't have to leave?" She tensed, holding her breath, waiting for him to push her away.

Instead, he sighed. "They said they were Siamese twins."

"And that they'd die if we tried to separate them."

"I remember."

Sarah's image became clear and sharp in Abby's mind. She watched her daughter move across the screen of memory as though she were watching through a window as Sarah played nearby, and she smiled. "How about the time she painted her stomach with glue and then put glitter on it. Remember? She ran around telling everyone that she was a jewel?" Abby could smell the scent of glue on Sarah's body, feel the roughness of the glitter against her hand. "I was vacuuming glitter for weeks."

"Oh yeah. I'd forgotten that one." He paused again, and when he spoke his voice was broken by a rising sob, as strange to her as the cry of an exotic bird. "I'm forgetting her, Abby. I feel like I'm starting to forget."

"Because we never talk about her."

"I know." He rubbed his eyes. "God, she was so fucking smart. Remember when your mom complimented her on her beautiful shoes, and she said, 'Actually, Grandma, they're sandals. But thank you nonetheless.' What was she then? Two?"

"Something like that." Abby raised her head, resting it in the cradle of her hand so she could see Michael's face as she spoke. The pictures were moving faster now, racing through her mind in a montage of memories. "Remember when you took her on that roller coaster, and she laughed so hard she peed?"

"And I almost threw up."

"And then she wanted to do it again."

"Yeah."

"And remember how she used to sit in the sandbox and eat sand by the handful?"

"Disgusting." He pushed her away and sat up. "It's so fucking unfair, you know?"

Abby nodded. "I know."

"Not her death. I mean, that, too, of course. But you!

You had so much more time with her than I did! I was working every goddamn minute, seeing my patients, going to analysis, *building my career.* Because there'd be time later, right? While you were with her all day long. Well, at least some days. So now you've got all these memories, and I've got nothing." He laughed bitterly. "What a fucking rip-off."

"You have memories, too. You just refuse to think about them."

"Because it hurts too much."

The room was quiet for a while. Then Abby spoke. "Don't you think that maybe we have to let it hurt, before it can stop?"

"I don't know," he said. "How the hell should I know?" He leaned against the headboard and pulled her close again.

Abby closed her eyes. "Well," she said, "you *are* the doctor."

"Physician, heal thyself." He shook his head. "Easier said than done, I guess. And what about you? You're a doctor, too."

" 'Physicians, heal each other'?" she suggested.

"How 'bout 'Physicians, have a margarita'?"

She laughed. "Frozen, no salt, and thank you very much."

Their laughter ebbed together. "Remember the time we drank those margaritas on the beach?" Michael said.

"I do. And I remember what happened *after* we drank those margaritas on the beach."

She felt his hand begin to stroke her hair. "Maybe we can get your mom to watch Ben one night this summer, when we're on the Vineyard."

"That would be great."

"Only three more weeks till vacation." She heard his voice echo deep within his chest and remembered snuggling against her father the same way as he read her stories in the evening. "Have you told your patients yet?"

She closed her eyes, willing away the guilt she knew she would feel, leaving. "All but Miranda. I haven't figured out how to break the news to her."

"Well, you'd better do it soon."

"I will," she said. "Tomorrow." She did not imagine that Miranda would take the news well.

They lay like that for a long time. Abby struggled to empty her mind of thought. She felt filled with warmth, Michael's body beside her triggering neurons, delineating her own flesh. She felt drunk with the tickle of his arm brushing against her side, the smell of aftershave and soap. His eyes fastened on hers.

"You look like you would glow in the dark."

She touched her lips with the tip of her tongue. "Want to find out?" she said.

Chapter Eighteen

Miranda stands at the dayroom window and watches the coming of the rain. Low in the sky, heavy black clouds prepare to bleed tears. Lightning flashes, a gleam in the sky, and thunder crashes against her ear. All day she has felt the air through an open window, hot and moist, full to bursting with something it cannot long contain. It frightens her, this sky, but it is beautiful, too, and the beauty makes her sad.

At last the rain begins to fall, plump, pregnant drops that spatter against the sidewalk and send waves of people scurrying for shelter under awnings and overhangs. The king is dead, and she knows but does not quite trust that what she sees is only water, cool and good. She watches the drops splash and die against her window, separated from her face by the skin of glass that cradles her cheek.

"What's up?" The voice behind her is rough and she does not turn around. "Like you ain't seen rain before?" It is Freddy. She sees him as he presses his face next to hers against the glass.

She speaks without moving. "I like to watch the rain."

Freddy turns and pulls himself up to sit on the window-sill, his back to the storm. "Shit, this ain't nothing. Where I come from, in Puerto Rico, man, now *those* were storms. Rain so thick you couldn't see your hand in front of your face."

Miranda lifts her head and looks at him, waiting for him to go on.

"I'm serious, man. And if you're thirsty, right? You just go out your door and open your mouth. I bet you drink a gallon in 'bout half a minute."

"You'd get soaked," she says seriously.

"Fuck, yeah. But we didn't mind. Ten minutes later, the sun comes out, and poof, you be dry again."

Miranda pauses, considering. The rain is coming so heavy now that the window is awash. The buildings outside seem to sway on waves of raindrops. "I've never felt the rain," she says. "I don't think I have. Or not for a long, long time."

Freddy looks at her in amazement. "No shit? That's fucked-up, man. Ain't nothing like getting soaked in a rainstorm. Beats the showers around here—that's for sure." He jumps down and stands quietly beside her. Outside, the traffic slows. Horns blare, jousting with the thunder. A woman holds the hands of two small children, and they run, laughing, down the street, their raincoats billowing behind them like sails.

"I got an idea," he says. "You up for a little adventure?"

Miranda tenses, shakes her head *no*.

"Aw, c'mon. You don't even know what I'm talkin' about."

She remembers the snakes, but there are no words in her mind to tell her, and the memory feels far away. There is nothing to hold her down. She feels herself willingly floating up to join him. "What?" she asks.

He looks at her. "I'm takin' you to the rain. Want to go?"

The voice in her head is silent. The king is dead. *The king is dead. The king is dead. Long live the king.* She understands. She nods, barely moving her head.

"Great. Just follow me, but be cool. Act like we're going to see your doc, awright? But when we get to her office, keep going. Anyone talks to us, let me do the talkin'."

Miranda nods again and follows him out of the day-room and down the hall. Maybe he is taking her to a place where she will die, but truly, she does not think so. It occurs to her that maybe he is her friend, and the feeling she has inside might be nothing more or less than the giddy beginning of being free.

"Wait up!" she calls, and runs ahead to join him. To-gether, they walk past the bedrooms, the conference room, the doctors' offices till they reach the service elevator. Freddy reaches into his pocket and pulls out a key. "Don't ask," he tells her, and looking around to make sure that no one sees, he plunges the key into a lock above a button and gives it a twist. Immediately, the button lights up, and Freddy pushes it. "Let's get a drink," he says, and they stand by the water fountain until the elevator arrives. When the door opens, he grabs her hand and pulls her laughing and breathless inside, and then the doors close and the elevator starts to move.

When they emerge, they are in the hallway that leads to the rooftop patio, where the tall woman takes her sometimes for their talks. She questions Freddy with her eyes and he understands her look and laughs. "Don't worry. We ain't there yet. But we through the hard part. The rest be easy."

They walk together to the end of the hall. Freddy opens a heavy door and motions her through. Inside, the air is dusty and stale. Suddenly frightened, Miranda pauses.

"Come *on,* man. We almost there."

Miranda hesitates. The stairs before her seem to go up like stairs to an execution. It is an effort now, to remember her father's words. *Do not talk to strangers. Do not go with strangers.* But he is not a stranger. Still, she waits. Thin light filters down from a skylight above and she hears a noise that she suddenly realizes must be the splashing of the rain.

"You comin' or what?" Freddy snorts in disgust. He takes her hand and tugs her, pulling her behind him up the stairs. She does not struggle or resist. After two flights, the stairs end abruptly. They are at the summit. Miranda is breathing hard from the unaccustomed exercise. With a flourish, Freddy pushes open the last door. Immediately, Miranda feels cool, wet wind blowing against her face. The rain is everywhere, falling fast and dancing on the soft black tar of the roof. She stares at it in wonder. Freddy looks at her and smiles. "Here," he says, as proud as if he had created it all himself. Then together, they step outside into the day.

At first the rain feels sharp against her skin, like tiny darts piercing armor. She slides her hand along her arm until the drops lie smooth, and then she feels her flesh melt into the rain until she, too, is fluid. She opens her mouth to the water, tasting its sweetness, letting it wash over and inside her. She has never felt so clean.

Slowly at first, then faster and faster, she begins to twirl among the drops. Freddy laughs and takes her hands, grasping them in his, and together they begin to spin, arching back, their mouths open to the sky, pulling each other around in circles until they fall, dizzy and panting, into puddles on the ground.

They lie there together, the rain streaming down their faces, until the world stops spinning and is still. "See?" Freddy says. "Told ya."

Inside Miranda's head it is quiet. She does not think; she only feels the rain falling against her flesh like tiny kisses. Beside her, Freddy jumps to his feet. "Watch," he says, and she opens her eyes to behold him tearing off his shirt and beating on his chest with his fists while his stamping feet send splashes of water back up into the air. "Rain dance," he tells her. "C'mon. You try."

But she is watching him, her eyes fastened on the muscles in his chest, which bulge and flatten again as his arms swing up and down. He has nipples, too, smaller than hers, ringed with small black hairs. She remembers the warmth of his lips against hers and shivers, feeling suddenly cold. He is far away now, lost in the rhythms of his own strutting body, eyes closed, and she is alone.

Through the wire mesh of the fence that surrounds

them both, she sees that the sky has grown lighter. The rain is coming more gently now and she reaches up with both arms, grasping at the air, until at last the music in her mind lifts her up to join him in his dance.

After the rain there is sun. They shake themselves dry like puppies, and watch the drops of water fly off of their bodies to sparkle in the light.

"They gonna be pissed, y'know," Freddy says. "We gonna get punished and shit." When they step off of the elevator, she sees that he is right. They yell at her, words that she does not hear, and grab her arm to lead her to her room, but inside she is wet and fluid as the water that flowed through their fingers. Roughly they towel her hair and toss her dry pajamas to put on and she makes her eyes go glassy and still as the surface of a pond, reflecting their images while showing nothing of her depths.

"You stay here," they tell her. "Dr. Cohen will be in soon."

She knows they want her to be afraid, but she is not. She lies on her bed and watches through the window as the clouds roll across the sky, thinks, *I have drunk you in; you are part of me and I am part of you,* sees herself floating free through blue infinity, safe.

She is lying there still when Abby comes, lies still as the weight of the woman settles next to her on the bed. "Heard you had an adventure," the woman says, and looking up, Miranda sees that her eyes are bright. "Must have been fun. Want to tell me about it?"

Suddenly, Miranda finds that she does want to tell. The

words pour out of her like the rain, forming puddles in the air. "Whoa!" Abby says. "Slow down, kiddo," but she is laughing and Miranda laughs, too.

She feels good all that day and into the next, when the woman returns to her and says without warning that she has something to tell her, too. "In a few weeks I'll be going on vacation. I'll be gone. . . ."

I'll be going. I'll be gone. Miranda clings tight to her mother's leg screaming, *Mommy, don't go. Mommy, don't go,* but her mother kisses her head and pries open her fingers one by one and shoves her back and closes the door and is gone forever and forever and forever. She watches the flap-flap-flap of the woman's ugly mouth, flap-flap-flap like a dying fish gasping for air. *I'll be back,* her mother says. *I'll come back for you when I can,* but she goes forever and forever and forever. Miranda is falling backward into blackness. Her eyes rain tears and the woman reaches out to touch her, but her touch will scald and Miranda brushes her hand away. She closes her eyes and the woman is gone. When she opens them again she sees that the woman has been changed. She has shriveled, like the evil queen in *Snow White* turning into an ugly hag. She will be going, she says, but to Miranda she is already gone. Outside Miranda's ears the words go on and on until at last the woman leaves and there is silence once more.

That went well, Abby thought as she left Miranda's room. *Really, that went just great.*

After work, Abby went to meet Tom for a drink, dreading another difficult conversation. The fantasies of him that had filled her mind for weeks had broken like a fever the night of his party, and she would have been happy to let the whole episode simply fade away, but he was not going to let her off so easily. His voice on the phone had been filled with desire.

He was sitting in a booth, sipping his beer, when she arrived. He smiled in anticipation as soon as he saw her, and reached out to hold her hand as she slid onto the bench opposite his. "Hey there, elusive one," he said, leaning over to kiss her. "I've been thinking about you."

"Me, too," she said, pulling her hand away.

He sat back and took another sip of his beer. "That doesn't sound good."

A waitress came by, and she ordered a gin and tonic. When they were alone again, she said, "You'll never believe what Miranda did yesterday."

"Do tell."

Her voice sounded artificial in her ears as she told him about the great escape, and when she came to the end of the story she lapsed limply into silence. His eyes flickered upward, scanning her face, and he ran his finger along her hand before she pulled away again. "I'm sorry," she said. "I just can't."

Tom reached for the saltshaker and began sliding it back and forth across the varnished table. "Sure seemed like you could last week."

"I know. I'm sorry."

"Sorry." He paused. "What about the night in my apartment? I— God, I felt so close to you. I just wanted—"

"I know," she said again. "I can never tell you what that meant to me, being able to talk to someone like that."

"To someone."

"To you, Tom, to you."

It was his turn to pull away. He crossed his arms over his chest and stared at her. "And now? That's it? This is it?"

Before Abby could answer, the waitress came back with her drink. "Can I get you folks something to eat?" she asked.

"I don't think so," Tom answered. "I don't think we'll be staying that long."

The waitress placed a bar receipt between them on the table. "You all just pay whenever you're ready," she said.

"Here's the thing," Abby said when she had gone. "I'm married."

"As opposed to last week?"

"I'm married," she repeated. "And I have a son."

"And you're not that kind of a girl."

"I guess not. Maybe I thought I could be, but I can't." He started to speak, but she cut him off. "I don't even think I want to try." She watched a muscle twitch above his jaw and felt a flood of maternal tenderness for him. She wanted to stroke his cheek, ruffle his hair, comfort him as she might comfort Ben. She could tell him that he deserved better, that he would meet some beautiful young, twenty-something thing who would give him the love and attention he had coming, but instead she sat quietly, waiting for him to speak.

Finally, he took another sip of his drink and looked up. "If you say you hope we can still be friends, I'll pour my beer in your lap."

She laughed. "I won't say it, then," she said. "But I hope we can."

He drained his beer and wiped his mouth. "So long," he said, getting to his feet. "I've got to run."

So she sat alone, sipping her drink, and watching him go. She wanted to cry, for his pain and for Miranda's, but not for her own. Those tears had been shed. She was sorry for the pain she might have caused, but she also felt a rising tide of hope, like a sailor must feel when he sets his back toward land and love, and turns to face the horizon.

Chapter Nineteen

As soon as the doctor told him she was going on vacation, Jack knew that he had won. He had crouched like a panther for so long, *lying in wait,* keeping the faith, and now all would be rewarded. When the cat went away, the mouse would play. He had taken their bullshit, watched his girl grow dull and fat, played good and dead until they were lulled into a false sense of complacency. It was no more than his wife had done to him. He had learned his lesson well— they could say that for him. He had waited in the shadows all this time. Soon it would be his turn to shine!

But today he'd play the good boy. He'd just pay a little visit to his daughter, like any caring dad would do. He'd just see if he could spend a little quality time with his girl, maybe mention, if it should happen to come up, that the doc was ditching them both to go play on some island paradise with her own family, her perfect husband and 2.7 blond little kids—yeah, she had kids. He would be sure to tell Miranda about that, too. She would find that amusing, he was sure.

He stormed through work with clenched teeth. It was his job to help the fancy-suit lawyers learn how to use their computers. It never failed to amaze him. For all their years of law school, all they seemed to know how to do was push a button and then call him in a panic when something went wrong. *Help!* they whined. *My Westlaw isn't working!* Or, *I just deleted my main file, and oops, I forgot to back it up!* And, *Please, please help right now because the meeting is in fifteen minutes.*

Normally, he liked his job. It was fun to laugh at those suits and skirts who thought they were just oh so smart, and fun to hold their careers in his hands as he negotiated the inner workings of their misunderstood machines. But today he had no patience for any of it. When the new suit in corporate called with his seventeenth stupid question of the day, he had told him to just read the goddamned manual for a change, assuming he could read, and had slammed the phone down in his ear. Probably the crybaby had run right to his boss, who, with a wink and a nudge, would make him bow and scrape for days to make amends. Well, screw him. Screw them all. Jobs came and went, he well knew, and if this one went, there would always be another. Miranda was unique.

Instead of waiting around to get reamed, he left the office early, to find the streets still crowded with people. *Fucking lemmings,* he thought as he pushed his way through thickets of hot, smelly bodies into the darkness of the subway and waited on the platform for his train. The air was rank, like rancid soup. An old man shuffled by, the flesh of his bare legs eaten away by spreading sores oozing pus. The stench made Jack retch and draw back. He watched as the man began to cough, hacking up green goo that he spat onto the ground. *I love New York,* Jack thought. *This is what they should have in those commercials. Come see the city as it really is.* A garbled message blared over the loudspeaker. On the opposite track, an express train screeched to a stop and more people flooded onto the platform, pushing Jack closer to the edge. He peered into the darkness of the tunnel, searching for lights that might signal the arrival of a train, but saw nothing. Behind him, people pressed closer, their sweaty flesh plastering him with slime. These were his tax dollars at work. Private money for the public good. Well, fuck it. Let the rest of these idiots wait. He was going to walk.

Fighting his way back up the stairs, he felt like a salmon swimming upstream. He waited patiently in line at the token booth. "There's no B train," he said to the woman clerk when it was finally his turn. "I'm just going to walk. I'd like my money back, please."

"Sorry," said the clerk. "Unless there's an official delay of service, I can't give you no refund. You can go back through, if you want. Train should be here soon."

Jack tried to keep his voice calm. "Well, apparently there *is* a delay of service. I've been waiting fifteen minutes. I'd call that a delay, wouldn't you?"

"I'm sorry, sir. Unless there's an official announcement, there's nothing I can do. Please step aside and let the people buy their MetroCards."

There was that voice again, that calm, bored, I-don't-give-a-shit voice telling him that he had no choice. No, you can't get your money back; no, you can't get your daughter;

no, you can't keep me from walking out that door—and for *no good reason,* no reason at all, just because they had the power and he didn't. These women thought they ran the world. Well, he was done with that, once and for all. "I will be happy to step aside once you *give me my fucking refund!*" he yelled. "I paid my money to ride the train. There was no train. I did not ride. Ipso facto I paid for NOTHING. So give me back my goddamned money. NOW!"

"Sir, I need you to step aside. If you want, you can write a letter to the MTA and request a refund. That's all I can do." She turned to the person behind him in line. "May I help you, ma'am?"

Jack slammed his hand against the Plexiglas window. "I said I want my fucking money!"

"Here." The woman behind him was holding out a dollar and some coins. "Look, I don't blame you. Here's two dollars. Take it."

They were all in cahoots, the lot of them, each one ready to watch the back of the next. That was where they got their power, really. If only men were like that, watching backs instead of stabbing them. Well, fuck her. Fuck them all. He took the money and, with a sudden motion, threw it as hard as he could at the clerk's fat face. The coins slammed against the Plexiglas shield and scattered on the floor. "Have a nice day," he said, "all of you," and he walked up the stairs to the street.

In the end, the walk to the hospital did him good. He was sweaty as hell when he finally got there, but he felt all right. Finally, he was learning to stick up for himself. No more doormat, he. Let them just try to nicey-nice him again. Let them just try. On Tower Ten he was faced again with a herd of cows, corralled behind another Plexiglas fence. But these cows were trained. They greeted him by name. A parlor trick, he thought, designed to amaze but amounting to nothing.

"Here to see Miranda?" the redhead asked.

No, he thought. *I came for the food.* But he was willing to play the game just a few more days. It wouldn't be long now till Miri begged to come home. So he smiled and nodded, said, "Yes, please, thanks," and took a seat as he was told, like the good boy he was.

He watched as Red sauntered down the corridor toward Miranda's room, and watched as she hurried back alone.

"Anything wrong?" he asked.

"Oh, no." She smiled. "She must be in the dayroom." Like a frightened mouse she took off down the hall. You'd think they could keep better track of these kids, Jack thought. At home, he always knew exactly where his daughter was and exactly what she was doing. *That's* what he called supervision. *That's* what kids needed. Red scurried by again. *Great,* Jack thought. *She's probably gotten lured into some pimply-faced sex-crazed jock's room where she's doing God knows what.*

Red appeared again, her eyebrows drawn. "Where's my daughter?" Jack said.

"Let me just get her doctor," Red answered. "Someone will be with you in a minute."

Jack stood and stepped toward her, his finger extended inches from her face. "Listen, you. I don't want *someone.* I want my *kid.* And I want her *now."*

Red took a step back. At least *she* could tell who was boss. "Of course, Mr. Reynolds. It'll just be a minute."

But it was more than a minute, more than two, more than five. Jack watched the second hand sweep circles around the clock as the nurses rushed past like a swarm of buzzing bees in an increasingly frenzied dance.

Jack sank into his chair and shut his eyes. Immediately, images of dirt-stained hands appeared, muscled hands cupping his daughter's virgin breasts. He saw himself slamming his fist into the kid's freckled face, felt the sweet release of bone crunching beneath his fingers. When he opened his eyes again, the so-called doctor was standing in front of him, tall as a goddamned totem pole.

"We have a problem," she said.

"Damn right you do." And he wouldn't hesitate to sue, either. Anyone, *anyone,* touched his baby, they'd be paying through the nose—he could promise them that.

The totem pole crouched before him, her hand on the arm of his chair. *That's right,* he thought. *Kneel. You kneel before me, bitch.* "Maybe we should go into my office," she said.

"Oh, no." He wasn't falling for that. He wanted witnesses. "Whatever problem you've got, you tell me here."

She took a breath. "I told Miranda about my vacation this morning. Right before I told you."

"Vacation, right."

"She seemed quite upset. That's not unusual. Many kids who've been through the things Miranda has—"

"She hasn't *been through* anything. Not till you got your hands on her."

"Well, all right. But her mother—"

"Her mother was a bitch. Miri was *glad* when she left."

The doctor lady sighed. "Well, for whatever reason, then, Miranda did seem upset this morning when I told her I'd be leaving for a few weeks. I planned to stop by this afternoon, but I had an emergency, so . . ."

"So . . ." he echoed, mocking.

"Well, she seems to have left the hospital. Or at least this floor. She was here at the last check an hour ago, so we know she can't be far, but—"

The world exploded, spewing rage. Jack lunged at Abby, his hands wrapping tight around her throat. His guttural scream echoed down the hall. As his hands squeezed tighter he felt her muscles sag. His fingers around her neck seemed enormous and strange. And then there were other hands, strong hands pulling on his arms. He felt a needle pierce his flesh, and then peace. He sagged to the floor, every muscle twitching. As they lifted him into a wheelchair he heard a voice from far away, floating like a feather into his ear.

"Abby? Abby? Are you all right? What the hell are we going to do now?"

On the roof, the sky is a clear bowl of blue. Miranda lies on her back, the black tar warm against her skin, and watches the flight of birds overhead. A pigeon lands on the edge of the chain-link fence and looks at her, then takes off into the sky once more. Watching him soar, Miranda thinks that she would like to be a bird. She imagines herself gliding through the air, looking down on the people below, swooping loop-the-loops above their heads, safe in a flock, needing no one.

She remembers a song that Freddy sang the night before, humming it first to himself and then singing her the words when she asked.

> *Blackbird singing in the dead of night*
> *Take these broken wings and learn to fly*
> *All your life*
> *You were only waiting for this moment to arise*
> *You were only waiting for this moment to arise.*

Miranda laughs aloud. It is so obvious, yet she has never seen it before. She can be a bird! She can fly! She stands and grasps the fence, leaning back until her face is pointing toward the sky. At last she knows where her mother has gone, and she knows what the song is telling her. At last, her mother is ready for her. At last, her mother is calling her home. Her broken wings feel strong again; finally, her moment has come. "Mommy!" she calls. "Wait for me! I'm coming!"

Her hands grip tight to the metal fence as she begins to climb, her eyes turned upward toward the sky.

"We have to call the police," Tom said. Laurie had called him as soon as Jack had been subdued. "You need to file a report."

Abby was sitting in a chair, trying to drink a glass of water. Her hands trembled, shaking the cup and wetting her tweed trousers. When she spoke, her voice was hoarse. "Absolutely not." She coughed, and took another sip of water.

Tom got up and began to pace. Her eyes watched him

move, back and forth, like a pendulum on a clock. Their kiss seemed unreal, something seen in a movie rather than lived. She remembered the softness of his lips against hers. Now his lips seemed shrunken, pressed tightly against his teeth. "You need to file a report," he said again, lifting a hand to silence her as she opened her mouth to speak, "for two reasons. One, this guy is crazy. He's dangerous. And he knows where to find you. If we go to court, we could almost surely get a restraining order."

"And we know how useful those are," Abby said.

"And second," Tom went on, ignoring her, "don't kid yourself. He's going to use the fact that Miranda went AWOL to try to get her home. And he could very well win. If we don't file a report, he's going to argue that this so-called attack couldn't have been too serious, nothing to prevent him from having custody. Do you really want her living back with him?"

Abby rubbed her throat. "I can't do it," she said. "I just— Look. Can you imagine what that would do to Miranda? She's got a pretty powerful transference going, you know. In her mind, I *am* her mother. How do you think she'd react, to have me put her father in jail? It would destroy her. I just won't do it."

"And knowing that her father attacked you? What's that going to do?"

"She never has to know."

Tom ran his hands through his hair. Outside the office door, a line of ragged kids was beginning to form, waiting for meds. He watched them shuffle to the nurses' station, some loud, demanding, and others so passive they seemed not to exist. "You're thinking like a psychologist," he said.

"I take that as a compliment. You're thinking like a lawyer."

"Ditto. And you tell me, who knows more about the real world?"

"Depends which world is real. For Miranda, I'd say her reality is what happens in her mind."

Laurie knocked on the door. "They found her," she said.

"Oh, my God. Where?" Abby was already at the door.

"On the roof. They're bringing her down now. Someone saw her, apparently—through his window, I think. Across the street."

"The roof? How the hell did she get up there again? By herself?"

"I don't know," Laurie said. "But she seemed to be trying to jump."

"Oh, shit," Abby said. "But they got her in time?"

"Just."

"Thank God." She looked at Tom, a hint of a smile on her face. "Still think she's going home?"

"I don't know," he said, following Abby down the hall. "Let's wait and see, I guess."

Chapter Twenty

Miranda is getting dressed. Her blue jeans feel tight against her legs. She misses the weightless comfort of the hospital pajamas. Snapping the pants closed, she pinches the flesh of her stomach and tears come into her eyes. This morning she is going outside. There are no snakes. She will be with the doctor and she will be safe. Her father says she will go home with him and tonight they will listen to some music and have a treat like cookies. Miranda likes cookies. She likes to push them into milk until they are soft and melt sweet and soggy on her tongue. She thinks about eating cookies with her father. They are laughing and he is stroking her hair and saying *You are my good girl, Miri, my good little girl,* and the air in the kitchen is warm and still. But the doctor says *You could stay here. What do you want?* Miranda thinks, *You do not know what you want,* and her chest falls in on itself until it is hard to breathe and the doctor says, *It is all right, you don't have to know, there are people that care about you who will decide what is best.*

She is pulling on her shirt and it is tight against her

chest. Her breasts have grown. They ache from the tape she has strapped tightly against them and still they grow. Perhaps the doctor is making them grow so that Miranda will be like her and stay with her and leave her father. It makes her angry to think that, and she beats her fists against her breasts until they are sore and she is crying. She does not want to go outside and she does not want to stay here and she does not want to be at home with her father. *You do not know what you want,* she thinks again, and then she curls up on her bed and looks at her fingers. They stand stiff and straight and strong before her eyes, yet they bow to her because she wills it. In her mind, she remembers the sky, and the flight of the almost bird she could have been. Her mother is not in the sky. She looks at her fingers for a long time and then the doctor comes to the door and says *All right, Miranda, time to go.*

Her feet scrape the tile as they move down the hall together. Natalie is there and says *Good luck, kid. We're rooting for you,* and Miranda thinks of blind piglets rooting for their mother's teats. She pulls back against the doctor's hand as Natalie says *Well, fuck you, too, if that's the way you gonna be.* The elevator door is open and *Here we go,* the doctor says as Miranda closes her eyes and allows herself to be led.

In the elevator there is noise and people talking. She hears a child cry and a woman says *You stop that—be good now or no candy after* and the crying stops and another woman says *You get over here now—I told you* and the woman's voice is hard.

"We need to get out now," the doctor says. "I want you to open your eyes."

Miranda opens her eyes and sees the sun shining down

through the large glass door. There is a man in a wheelchair who is crooked and shaking. He leans toward her and shakes faster and faster and she wants to run because he is casting a spell on her and soon there will be snakes. She breaks free of the doctor's hand and turns back toward the elevator, but the doctor catches her hand and says *You will be all right. Come on, we need to go now.* Then they are outside with noises all around, snorts and shouts and laughter, and Miranda tries to take herself far away, but the doctor is holding her hand and she cannot go, so she stays in her body as they get into the hot black car and drive away. She likes the car. It is safe, like being inside outside, because the scary things are through the window and they are moving so fast that they cannot catch her. She lets go of the doctor's hand and remembers riding long ago on a big, big bus as she knelt on a hard-backed seat beside a woman who told her she'd be safe, and watched the world go by outside the window.

Abby felt the warmth of the girl's body and resisted the urge to reach out and stroke her shining hair. A part of her wished that she could tell the driver to turn around. She could give him her address, secrete Miranda away with her. Michael wanted another child—why not this one? Together they could bring her back to life, and Ben would love to have a sister. Embarrassed by her own thoughts, Abby turned away from Miranda and looked out the window at the city, derelict buildings and sweat-sheened bodies flashing past behind the glass. Despite herself, the words formed in her mind: *it would be so good to have a daughter.*

At last the car stopped. Manhattan State Hospital, a

hulking white behemoth, towered before them. "What time will you need the pickup?" asked the driver.

Abby shrugged and looked at her watch. "Two o'clock, maybe? Can I call you?"

"No problem."

Abby turned to Miranda and tugged gently on her hand. "We're here," she said. "You ready?" There was no response. Gently, Abby pulled the girl to her feet and led her through the gray hospital doors toward the courtroom inside.

Jack jumped out of his taxi and bounded up the white stone steps to the hospital. Inside, a phalanx of people in ragged clothes circled around him, drooling, blinking. They stood too close and talked too fast. "Hey, mister, got a quarter? Got a dollar? Got a million dollars?" There was laughter and the stench of bodies. He stepped forward, more angry than afraid. *This* was where they were bringing Miranda? His princess child? He shouldered his way to the elevator and went to the fifth floor, where he would meet his lawyer. He was not afraid of losing. He was an educated man. This was still America; people still had rights. Maybe in Russia they could take your child away for no reason, but not here. His lawyer agreed. All he had to do was stay calm. Just play the game, and Miranda would be going home with him that afternoon.

Unless, he thought. Unless the goddamn doctor had gotten her head all turned around. Unless that arrogant bitch who thought she knew what was best had been able to brainwash his innocent child. He began to pace in the corridor, trying to block the anger he felt rising within him. He had promised his lawyer he would be calm. Where was his lawyer, anyway? He was late. Jack hated that. He himself made a point of being early for appointments. It was a simple matter of courtesy. He drummed his fingers against his thigh. *Let's get this show on the road,* he thought.

He was still pacing when he saw them get off the elevator. Miranda looked different, out of her hospital pajamas. Her clothes were tight against her. He could see her breasts, straining at the thin fabric of her T-shirt. Her jeans bulged at the waist, as though they could not contain the flesh within. Hadn't he taught her to dress properly? She was disgusting. He wanted to slap her. And the look on her face: no more the innocent girl who waited for him at home. The doctor had done her work.

"Miranda!" he called, and she looked up at him without letting go of the doctor's hand.

"Daddy."

"Come here." He took off his jacket and draped it over her shoulders. Remembering to keep his voice calm, he said, "That's better. We don't want to cause a riot now, do we?"

"No, Daddy."

Abby joined them. "I guess she put on some weight in the hospital. I should have asked you to bring different clothes."

"Yes, you should have."

"Maybe later this week—"

Jack cut her off. "Later this week she'll be home with me."

Abby tried to smile. "Well, we'll see."

"Yes, we will."

Abby put her hand on Miranda's arm. "It's time to go in."

Miranda paused, looking at her father. "Daddy?"

Jack felt himself relax. She still belonged to him, after all. "You go ahead," he said. "I'll see you inside."

The hospital's courtroom was large and square, low-ceilinged, with long fluorescent lights that illuminated the grime on the walls and floor. Along one wall, someone had scrawled GIVE ME LIBERTY OR GIVE ME DEATH in indelible black marker. A small, bedraggled American flag hung opposite. In the corner, a large fan stirred the dust, and lawyers conferred with dead-eyed patients in quiet voices. The judge sat on his dais, behind a large wooden desk. Beads of sweat collected against his graying hair. He yawned, rubbed his eyes, then began to arrange a stack of paper clips on his desk. "It's hot," he said aloud, to no one in particular. Then, as though suddenly aware that people were watching him, he straightened in his chair. "Are we ready? What's next? Let's keep it moving, shall we?"

A man in a blue suit placed a pile of papers on the judge's desk and spoke to him in a low voice. "All right," boomed the judge. "The matter of St. Ann's versus Reynolds. Everybody here? Everybody ready?"

Abby saw Tom stand and nod toward the judge. She remembered their kiss, and a painful flush of shame suffused her face. Her body felt heavy, pressing into the seat. "Yes," she heard Tom say. They were ready to proceed.

The judge slid on a pair of wire-rimmed glasses and scanned the paper in front of him. "All right. As I understand it, we have a minor child, Miranda Reynolds, who was found in the park on April tenth and brought to St. Ann's. Been on the inpatient unit ninety-plus days, recent suicide attempt. Father is petitioning for custody; hospital wants her declared PINS and remanded to their care for an additional sixty days. Is that right?"

"Yes, Your Honor," said Tom. "We feel that the suicide attempt suggests she continues to present a danger to herself."

"Convince me," said the judge.

Tom stood behind his table as he explained in a pleasant, conversational tone the circumstances surrounding Miranda's admission to the hospital. "On the evening of April tenth, Miranda was left unsupervised in her apartment."

"Unsupervised?" interrupted the judge. "How old is she?"

"She's twelve, Your Honor."

"So how much supervision does she need? You tell me you can't leave a twelve-year-old unsupervised, and we'll have to get them all taken away from their parents. No one could stand to be with a twelve-year-old all the time." His laugh boomed into the silent courtroom.

"Yes, Your Honor. But the results of the psychological testing will show a mental age equivalent of approximately eight years old, with marked delusions and paranoid features. It is our belief that her father knew, or should have known, that Miranda was incapable of caring for herself."

"So what? Why was she unsupervised that day? Was the babysitter late, or what?"

"She was unsupervised every day. The girl was alone in the apartment five days a week."

The judge leaned forward and grabbed a handful of paper clips, then let them dribble slowly through his fingers. "Let me try to understand. She was too sick to be unsupervised on April tenth, but on April ninth, and April eighth, and all of the other days before that, she got along fine by herself. Is that what you're saying?"

"If you'll just let me continue, Your Honor."

"Please."

Abby looked away, wishing she could close her ears as easily as avert her eyes. As she heard Tom outline the rest of their case, the lack of schooling, the long hours alone, the obvious psychological and emotional problems, the lack of appropriate parenting, a feeling of helplessness welled up inside her. Miranda had been better off with Jack after all. Happier, more at peace. It was only on her watch that Miranda had tried to hurt herself. At home she had been disturbed, but safe. They were going to lose. And then she heard her name being called, and she went to get sworn in.

Dutifully, in response to Tom's questions, she stated her name, her position, her training, and her qualifications, and then began to deliver the results of the psychological evaluation and her clinical assessment of Miranda. She looked at the girl, wondering how much she could understand, wishing that she could be spared this last betrayal: that Abby Cohen, her doctor, did indeed think she was insane.

But Miranda is far away, and the words mean nothing. She is on her island warm in the sun, with a cool breeze blowing on her face. She is naked and laughing when she looks down to see a hard, smooth chest and a penis between her legs. Her father is there and hugging her, telling her she did it, she did it, and crying with joy. *It is safe now,* he tells her. *I will take you home, but you can be with her, too, the doctor, your mother. You can go to school and float in trees and fly through the air on a swing because now you will be safe.* And then her father is gone and the penis is gone and she is herself again, wounded, bleeding, rotting inside, oozing pus, and the doctor is gone. Miranda whimpers to herself. She wants them all to go away and not call her. They are calling her. She does not want to answer. She wants to lie still in the sun and watch the green leaves above her as the sunlight filters down in moving patterns on the water.

She opens her eyes and they are looking at her, calling her with their eyes. She shakes her hair in front of her face and they are gone.

On the witness stand, Abby was describing all she knew of Miranda's life at home: the long, empty days spent with folders of work sheets, the sameness of meals consumed alone in the kitchen, long afternoons spent lying on her bed, lost in fantasy. From his seat at the table, Jack listened, enraged. So the girl had told. Away from him for a few months, she had belched up the secrets of their life so that they could be used against him in a court of law. And the doctor up there now, making all he had done sound sordid and evil, when what had it been? He had kept her safe, safe and happy. He leaned over to his lawyer. "There were no locks on the door. Just tell them that. She could have walked out anytime. All she would have had to do was say, 'Daddy, I want to go to school.' I would have signed her up in a second. But she said she didn't want to go. She wanted to stay inside. Tell them that, okay? Tell them that."

"Shhhhh," the lawyer said. "We'll get our chance. Just relax. The calmer you are, the better we'll do."

Jack nodded. Right. Stay calm. His lawyer stood, and moved toward Abby. "To the best of your knowledge, was Miranda ever locked inside the house?"

"Not to the best of my knowledge, no. But there are other ways—"

"Just yes or no, please. Was she tied up? Chained? Restrained in any way?"

"No, but—"

"Beaten? Threatened?"

"I don't really know."

"But Miranda never told you of any beatings or threats?"

"No."

"And she never tried to kill herself before she came to the hospital, did she?"

Abby felt the sting of his words sharp in her ear. Her eyes blurred with tears. "No," she said, miserably, "not that I know of."

"But she did try to commit suicide once in your care, did she not?"

"Yes . . . she did become suicidal. That's exactly why we feel she needs continued hospitalization."

"Let me understand what you're saying. If a person shows no suicidal tendencies in a home environment, and then attempts suicide after three months of hospitalization, while still in the hospital, your recommendation would be continued hospitalization?" He laughed and shook his head. "Doesn't make much sense to me, but then, you're the doctor."

Tom got to his feet. "Objection, Your Honor. Is there a question there?"

The judge peered at Jack's lawyer. "Is there something else you'd like to ask this witness?"

"No, Your Honor," Jack's lawyer said. "Nothing further."

Abby walked back to her seat. "Sorry," she whispered to Tom.

He shrugged. "Maybe Dad will lose it during the cross."

Jack had taken the witness stand and was being sworn in. Leaning forward in the chair, his stiff gray hair standing up like dead grass on a riverbank, he looked like a picture of a responsible parent. He stated his name and address, acknowledged that he was Miranda's father, and said that he had been her sole caretaker for the past six years, since her mother had died.

"Can you describe your life with Miranda over those years?" the lawyer asked.

Jack settled back in his chair. "Well, right after her mother died, it was a terrible time for both of us." He paused, shifting his eyes between the judge and his lawyer. When he spoke again, his voice was smooth, like oil on a burn. "We were both in pain, in shock really. It had happened so suddenly. Maybe I made a mistake in keeping Miranda home from school those first few weeks. In hindsight, I should have made her go, right away, gotten her back on the horse and all that, but she was so unhappy. I'd pack her lunch in the morning and try to get her out the door, but then she'd cry and beg me not to make her leave. I just didn't have the heart."

"I understand," said the lawyer.

"Make me puke," Abby whispered to Tom. She had never seen Jack look so calm and sane. A true sociopath, she thought. The mass-murdering psycho of whom the neighbors would say on the news, *He seemed like such a nice boy.* Beside her, Miranda sat staring down at her hands, which lay crossed in her lap. "Are you okay?" Abby asked, but Miranda did not respond.

Miranda hears her father's voice float over her on the warm breeze, and it tastes like syrup in her mouth, sweet at first and then too sweet, coating her tongue, swelling her throat, making her feel afraid. The voice is talking about her mother but Daddy said the woman was not her mother because she was bad and they should not cry for her but now she was good and they were sad and they should cry and she should cry but the woman was not her mother because she was bad. She looks up and sees her father sitting in the chair and his mouth is moving, but it is not him talking, and she is afraid because maybe he is dead and maybe he is a robot and maybe if she goes home with him the robot will kill her as he has killed her father. The woman beside her is stiff and may be her mother or maybe not, and Miranda feels frightened and looks down again at her fingers and maybe no place is safe, after all. Then the words are sounds again like music, without meaning, and her father's voice is soft as the wind and he loves her because she is his little girl, and the music covers her like a blanket warm and safe like at night, when she hides her head under the covers and the only sound is the sound of breathing, in and out, in and out, until she falls asleep.

"And then, of course, it was summer," Jack was saying. "I couldn't be home all the time, so I hired a woman to take care of her while I was at work. She told me they went outside every day, but looking back, I guess she was more interested in her TV than in keeping Miranda busy, because in the fall Miranda told me that she'd been in all summer. Now, in hindsight, it's easy to say I should have known, but you need to remember that I was pretty shaken myself. I'd just lost my wife, after all."

"And then what happened?"

"When school started, Miranda told me that she didn't want to go. She said the other kids were mean to her. Of course I told her she had to go, but . . . it was weak of me—I know that now—but I just couldn't stand the crying. Then I remember I was watching TV. I saw this show on home-schooling. And that's what we started. I'd plan out her studies for the year, then break it down into months, weeks, and days. She's up to grade level. Even the doctor will tell you that."

"Weren't you concerned, leaving a six-year-old alone in the house all day?"

"Actually, she was seven by then. Very mature. She's always been mature for her age. She knew not to light the stove, not to play with matches, not to open the door. What else was there for me to worry about?"

"And were there ever any problems? Any incidents that made you feel she couldn't handle the responsibility?"

"No, never. She was always happy to see me at the end of the day. Her work was done; the house was pretty neat. There were no problems." He laughed. "It was now, now that she was getting to be a teenager, that I was starting to get more worried. How much trouble can a seven-year-old dream up, right? And then, I tell you, it just got to be a routine. She was learning so much, she seemed to be doing well, she never wanted to go back to school, and I didn't mind the extra work if it made her happy. I tell you, time flies. It's hard for me to believe we've been doing it for five, almost six years now. It just got to be a routine."

Jack's lawyer strolled to the end of the room and back, his hands tucked casually in his pockets, before he continued. "During this time, did you notice any change in Miranda? Any fears? Any, ah, delusions?"

Jack shook his head. "Absolutely not."

"Did she ever mention a fear of snakes?"

"No."

"Ever talk about bad people who were trying to kill her?"

"No."

"Anything like that?"

Jack paused, as if deep in thought. "No. Not at all." He looked beseechingly at the judge. "I'm not saying she wasn't scared, but she never said anything to me. I mean, now I see that she must have been afraid of something. But I'm telling you, the days went by so fast, and then in New York, you know, it's always too hot out or too cold or then raining or something, and we always had enough to do to keep us busy. It's a funny thing, you know? You don't really think about your life—you just live it. And this got to be our life. If I'd ever thought she was afraid, well, I'd have taken her outside myself, to show her there was nothing to be scared of. But she never said anything about—what was it, snakes? Why would you be scared of snakes in New York City?"

Yes, why would you? thought Abby. *Why would it ever occur to you to be scared of something you had never even seen, unless someone told you that you had to be?* She looked at the judge, trying to gauge his reaction to Jack's testimony, but his eyes were focused on his desk and she could not read his expression. Miranda was staring at her father with glazed, unseeing eyes, and he returned her gaze.

Watching him watch his daughter, Abby could see real love in his eyes. She had seen it whenever he looked at her, whenever he pulled her robe closer around her shoulders, or leaned down to kiss her hair. It was the same look Michael wore on his face when he tucked Ben into bed at night. For the first time, she felt she understood him. In his own crazy way, he had been doing only what any parent did, what she had tried to do and failed. He had been trying only to keep his child safe. This sudden knowledge filled her with an aching sense of kinship. *I know you,* she thought. *I understand.*

On the witness stand, Jack had finished his testimony, and Tom rose to cross-examine him.

"So it never seemed odd to you that your daughter never went outside, not once in five and a half years?"

Jack ducked his head respectfully. "If you put it like that, yeah, I guess it does, but with us it was just day by day, living normal. What do I know about kids? She's the only one I got, and I tried to do my best by her."

"You're an educated man, correct?"

"I graduated cum laude from St. John's."

"So surely you understand the importance of regular medical care."

"Miranda was never sick."

"Did you ever take her for a checkup? For immunizations?"

"She was never sick."

"I see. And you never thought she might need friends? Kids her own age that she could play with?"

"She never said she wanted any. She seemed happy."

"Look at your daughter, Mr. Reynolds. Does she seem happy now?"

Jack's eyes followed Tom's finger to where Miranda sat, head down, pale and frozen. "No, of course she doesn't. That's exactly my point. You all have traumatized her for months, kept her away from her own father, dragged her here to court. Don't blame me if she's miserable. She was happy enough with me."

"Then why did she leave?"

"She got scared—that's why. I was stuck on the subway one night on my way home, so I was late. She went out to try to find me and she got lost. I should sue you sons of bitches," he added under his breath.

"When she got to the hospital, she was talking about snakes and bad men who were out to get her, about how it wasn't safe to go outside."

"She was scared."

"She was psychotic."

"That's your opinion."

"That's the opinion of the doctors on Miranda's unit."

"Who have known her for a few months. I've known her for almost thirteen years, her whole life. I'm her father, for crying out loud. Don't you think I know what's best for her?"

Tom stood in front of Jack and looked directly into his eyes. "So you see nothing wrong with Miranda, emotionally?"

"Nothing that a father's love won't fix."

"And if she is released to you, you'll go back to the same . . . routine?"

Jack looked at his lawyer. "There will be some changes. We'll get a phone, for one, so that she can reach me if she needs me. If she tells me she wants to go to school, she'll go. If not, I'll . . . hire someone to come be with her for part of the day while I'm at work. I guess it's possible that she might have been a little lonely before. But she never said anything, so how could I know?"

"But you don't feel that her emotional problems require treatment?"

Again, Jack's eyes focused on his lawyer. "I'd be open to the possibility of getting some therapy for her. Maybe she's never gotten over her mother's death. I don't know. I'd be willing to consider it, if Miranda wanted it. On an outpatient basis."

Abby shook her head. It seemed to her that Tom had done a great job of proving Jack Reynolds' case. His lawyer had done a good job with him.

Tom asked a few more questions, and then Jack stepped down. The courtroom was quiet, except for the humming of the fan in the corner. The air felt old, already used. Abby yawned, fighting the drowsiness she knew masked unbearable tension. All right, so Jack loved Miranda. All right, he had only been trying to do his best. But his best meant enslaving Miranda to his needs, while obviating her own. She hoped the judge would see that only Abby could set her free. She could not bear to lose another child, this child.

On the dais, the judge stuck a paper clip in his ear and rolled it back and forth, then took it out and looked at it. He tossed it in the garbage under the desk and scribbled some notes on a yellow pad. "All right," he said. "Let's take a short recess, and then I'd like to meet with Miranda in my chambers. Alone." He banged his gavel on the desk as though he enjoyed the noise it made, and said in a booming voice, "Court adjourned."

Miranda is taken by the hand and led into a small room where a man in black sits behind a desk, and a woman with a strange box sits beside him. The man's hair is white, and she watches him rub at it where it grazes against his ear. Her father's hair is gray and stiff. The man is called a judge, the doctor said, and he will know what is best for her but it will help if she can tell him what she wants. *You do not know what you want. My name is Judge Carey,* the man says. *What is your name?* In her head she hears the word *Miranda* but the room is still and she knows the sound did not last outside her mouth but died within her. *Can you tell me your name?* he asks again, this man with drops of water on the side of his face, and she thinks of a glass filled with apple juice and ice that bled tiny clear beads onto the wooden table in her room and her father said *Bad, clumsy girl you stupid Miranda get a towel get a coaster we don't put glasses on our good wood table Miranda Miranda hurry up you may have ruined it* as he says again *There's nothing to be afraid of you can tell me your name.*

"Miranda," she says, and she hears it in the room.

"Ah, good. Miranda. What a pretty name."

His mouth opens and his voice is in the room but his voice is low like water splashing hard and fast out of the bathtub tap and the words are music in her ears: *So why are we here well we're here to decide what will be best for you, what will be best for Miranda, because that's all that matters, not what is best for your father or the doctors or anyone else, do you understand?* The voice stops and she looks up and looks down and the voice goes on: *Good because maybe we can decide together and you can tell me what you want (you do not know what you want) can you tell me what you want.*

In her mind, Miranda sees herself sitting in the kitchen, working on the problems her father has left for her cool and stiff in their creamy folder, and the numbers are safe as she moves them back and forth, writing carefully in black pencil on the clean white pages, and she is alone with the numbers, with the silence in her ears like wads of cotton, sealing her off, and then she is lying on her bed and there are no dead-beaver girl and no checkers and no voices around her like music as she eats her sandwich and they are rooting for her and she is rooting, rooting like a newborn pig, and there are snakes in the world and her father needs her and the doctor her mother will live with them and take care of her and she will be little again and unafraid, pumping her legs on the swing as the wind rushes back and forth past her ears. But the voice is in her ears: *Do you want to go back to your father because you can but you don't have to if you don't want to you know that all you have to do is tell me what it is that you want Miranda you don't have to be afraid and no one will hurt you and no one will know what you tell me here it will be our secret just between us.*

She looks at him then and sees his face pale and round and flat like a picture of the moon in her storybook at home and he is the man in the moon who will watch her at night and keep her safe and she smiles at him and sees the smile reflected on his face.

"That's better," he says. "There's a girl. Now tell me, did your father ever do anything to hurt you?"

And she sees her father coming in and she is running to hold him and feels his arms around her gentle and strong and *only bad men hurt Miranda*. He says *There are bad men in the street but I will keep you safe* and of course her father would not hurt her, she thinks, but if he did then there would be a reason, and she sees him hit her mother hard across the face, but her mother was bad, and it hurts to look at the picture, so she closes her eyes and shakes her head back and forth so that her hair is in front of her eyes.

"Okay," says the judge. "And are you afraid of him? Has he ever threatened you? Said he would hurt you in any way?"

Miranda looks at his face and he is the man in the moon shining through her window. "My father says he will keep me safe. He takes care of me."

"What are you frightened of?" he says, and she sees them in front of her eyes, snakes spitting white, and she closes her eyes.

Then the deep voice is in the room: *It's okay. You don't have to tell me. It's all right. Are you all right?* But she is trying to leave, squeezing her eyes shut and pressing herself back into the chair, and there is another noise in the room that sounds like pain, a whimpering sound, and then the music of the deep voice saying *Bailiff, bailiff, let's get her back to Dr. Cohen, thank you Miranda you have helped us a lot you can go now are you ready to go,* but as they lift her arms and guide her from the room she is already gone.

The bailiff preceded them into the courtroom. "All rise."

The judge pointed to Abby, and motioned for her to take Miranda back to her seat. Abby jumped to her feet. Perhaps they had won, after all. She wondered what Miranda had said to the judge. Taking Miranda's limp hand in hers, Abby led her back to their chairs. Miranda's head slumped over her chest and her hair covered her eyes.

The judge cleared his throat and began to speak. "It is my impression that Miranda Reynolds is indeed suffering from a mental illness, and must receive ongoing psychiatric and/or psychological treatment."

Abby grinned at Tom and grabbed his hand. "We did it!" she mouthed.

"However," the judge continued, "it is also clear that,

at this time, Miranda does not present an immediate danger to herself or to others. With proper supervision, there is no reason why she could not be maintained at home, and receive such care on an outpatient basis. Since Mr. Reynolds has provided for her care adequately in the past, there is no reason why he should be denied custody now. I therefore remand Miranda to her father's care, and order that she be seen by Dr. Cohen for psychological care not less than once per week. I would also strongly encourage you, Mr. Reynolds, to enroll Miranda in a special education class as soon as possible. I will assign a social worker to you, to help you with any problems that might arise." He banged his gavel on the desk. "Court adjourned."

Tom put his hand on Abby's arm. "Could have been worse. At least you can still treat her."

"Yeah." Abby felt tired. *If* Miranda could articulate her need, and *if* Jack followed through, she could still see Miranda once in a while. Their work would be no more than etchings in the sand, washed away by the ocean of Jack's pathology. "If he brings her."

"He'll have to," Tom said, "if he wants to keep her."

In her chair on the other side of Abby, Miranda was still. She gave no indication that she heard the judge, or understood what was going to happen. Abby turned to her. "You're going home with your father, after all."

Miranda gave no response. It fell to Abby now to reassure the girl, to give her a talisman against the darkness she felt closing in. "It will be all right," she said. "Your father will take good care of you, and if you want, we can still see each other once a week. Tell your father you want to see me.

He'll bring you to my office in a taxi." She was rambling, her voice floating like vapor past Miranda's silent frame.

Miranda is trying to leave, but she cannot find her way. Her mother-not-mother is beside her and she is telling her she must go to her father, but that is not what she wants, and suddenly she knows what she wants. She calls out to them all, screaming in her mind that she wants to stay with her mother in the place of stitched-together days, but the air around her is filled only with the woman's voice, and she is saying *Look, Miranda, your father is here. It's time to say good-bye.*

Jack was standing in front of them. "Miri! We won! We won! I get to take you home." He took her hand. "Thank you," he said to Abby. "Thank you for all your help."

Abby pushed her mouth into a smile. "I look forward to seeing you soon, and Miranda. Should we try to make an appointment now?"

Jack took a step back. "I'll call."

"You do that."

Abby felt the air rush from the room and she struggled to catch her breath. *Don't cry,* she told herself. *Keep it professional.* "I'll see you, Miranda. Take care."

"Don't worry about a thing," Jack said. Gently, he tugged on Miranda's hand, thinking, *See you NOT, you asshole, because I'll be damned if you ever see my daughter again.* "Come on, Miri," he said as he led her away. "It's time to go home."

Abby watched her go, wishing she could reach in and hold her as Jack pulled her across the room. "I love you," she said to Miranda's back, knowing it was wrong, wanting to yell *Don't go,* to run after her and snatch her away and hold her close forever. Her eyes burned with a fire of tears. Miranda was not her child after all. She was not even her patient.

Miranda is swimming through the water, holding her father's hand. She is going home with her father, home where it is safe and still, but she hears the sound of fabric ripping, sees her flesh tear like a sheet caught in a bedspring, and looking back over her shoulder, she screams, "Mommy! Mommy!" But the sound is in her head and not in the room, and her father leads her gently by the hand back out into the street, and into a taxi to take them home.

Chapter Twenty-one

The low stone walls lay like scars across the weathered face of the land. They had arrived on the ferry that morning, Abby and Michael and Ben, and had driven off the boat into the gray fog that often shrouded the Vineyard until noon. As they drove west across the island, the crush of cars that had surrounded them near the harbor grew sparse. Many people came to Martha's Vineyard for the fancy shops and restaurants that populated the eastern end of the island, but Abby had always loved the wilder western tip, where her house lay. The road they traveled wound past scrubby pastures and meadows so thick with wildflowers that you could barely see the grass. The fields sloped gently down for miles, all the way to the sea, but today it was hard to make out even the outlines of the white clapboard farmhouses that stood shaded by trees a hundred years old. As they passed the old wool mill a flock of sheep looked up from their grazing to follow the movement of the car with mild eyes. Overhead, the sun was a blazing disk in the sky, struggling to burn through the mist. It was going to be a beautiful day.

She opened her window and breathed the moist air.

"Mmmmm," she said. "Smell the ocean, Ben?"

Strapped into his car seat and clutching his ragged blue stuffed elephant, Ben nodded. "I want to go to the beach. Can we, Mom?"

I want to go to the beach. Can we, Mom? Abby remembered herself asking the same question as they made this drive each summer, remembered her sister and her sitting in the backseat, straining against their seat belts, fighting to be the first to glimpse the water, the first to see the lighthouse that guarded the Gay Head cliffs, begging to be taken to the beach while the grown-ups mouthed those awful words *Be patient.* The sweet tang of the bubble gum her parents used to bribe her into compliance on these trips filled her mouth. How strange it was to be the adult, keeper of rules, setter of priorities. Her son was bouncing in his car seat. "Can we, Mom? Please?"

She had not forgotten how hard it was to wait. "We'll change into our bathing suits the minute we get to the house."

Ben threw his elephant into the air. "Yea!"

They stopped at the Chilmark store to buy milk, juice, bread, eggs, and pasta, enough to last them through lunch. Later, Abby would go do a "big shop" at the up-island Cronig's, but it would be easier to do that without Ben. Besides, she had always loved this store, despite the outrageous prices. She breathed in the aroma of pizza and fresh doughnuts, fingered the silky ears of corn still cool in their wooden basket, listened to the slap of the screen door against its frame and the jingle of the little bell that announced yet another customer. She would have loved to buy herself a *Times* and a cup of coffee and enjoy them in one of the oversized rocking chairs out on the porch, as she and Michael had done in the early, prechild years of their courtship and marriage. But Ben wanted to get to the beach. She paid for her purchases, buying three pieces of Bazooka bubble gum on a sudden impulse with fifteen cents of her change, and went to find her son.

Outside on the porch, Ben stood alone, gently fingering his elephant while he watched older kids, tanned and hard-bodied in their cutoff shorts, teasing each other and laughing, their mouths full of doughnuts. He seemed to be studying them as an anthropologist might study a distant civilization. "They're teenagers, Mom," he said, his voice full of awe, as Abby took his hand. Abby, used to the hospital shuffle and tortured faces of the kids on Tower Ten, was awed, as well. How effortlessly they seemed to inhabit their bodies, to own the space in which they stood. How easy they made it seem, being young.

One of the girls had long, straight brown hair, which she pushed back from her face as she spoke. *Miranda,* Abby thought, and then turned away as if in pain. She handed her son a piece of bubble gum and he gave her a surprised and happy smile. "C'mon, sweetie. Let's go. The sooner we get these groceries home, the sooner we can go to the beach." *How Miranda would love it here,* she thought. She pictured her running down the beach, feeling the squish of the sand between her toes and the shock of cold water against her skin, with nothing between herself and the natural world.

Ben slid his fingernail under the wrapper of his gum. "For later, right?" he asked doubtfully.

"Nope," she told him. "For right now. This is vacation, after all."

"Vacation!" he echoed. Michael called to them from the car, where he sat double-parked, at ten thirty on a Saturday morning. God, the island had gotten crowded. She sighed. No more thoughts about Miranda. She, too, wanted to go to the beach.

"Coming," she said, and guided her son carefully through the maze of bodies on the stairs.

Jack locks the door behind them and draws her to him in the silence. "Welcome home."

Pulling out of his embrace, she looks around the room and sees that everything is small and still and strange. She moves slowly to the table and fingers its smooth wooden surface, touches the pencils that stand stiff in their cup. These things were once filled with life; now they are dead. She sits heavily in the chair and sighs.

Her father's hand burns her shoulder. "Are you hungry, sweetheart? Want something to drink?"

She shakes her head no.

"No, thank you," he corrects, and she hears her whispered voice echo his words. Getting up, she walks away from him, into the living room. He follows her like a dog, watching, anxious, alert, stands behind her as she looks out the window at the traffic moving past outside. Only that has stayed the same, and it comforts her. Then the traffic blurs before her eyes and she sees Freddy dancing in the rain. She presses close to the glass to hide her smile.

Her father sees. "Happy to be home, huh? I bet! I'm happy to have you here, too. I missed you, sweetheart. I missed you so much. But now I've got you back, and you will never, never leave again."

You will never, never leave again. The words echo in her mind as Freddy fades into the swiftly moving cars below. Her father has won. He is the strongest, after all, and yet he hovers behind her. She can smell his fear and she sees with sudden clarity that what he fears is her. Her body swells with its newfound power, and she runs her finger down the cool glass, knowing that she could break it with a single flick of her nail against the pane. *A little knowledge is a dangerous thing,* she thinks. Behind her, she hears her father breathe. He is waiting for her.

Less than an hour after they had left the store, Abby was struggling down the path to the beach, juggling towels and toys, yelling at Ben to wait up and for God's sake not to go into the water until she got there. Michael had sent them on ahead, saying he would meet them after he had gotten things organized just a little bit, and Ben had been too excited to complain. The sun had finally broken through the mist, and the day was warm despite the ocean breeze. Watching her son scamper down the path ahead of her, Abby was suddenly aware of feeling happy. She had shed her city skin at last, and was coated only in suntan lotion and a thin film of sweat.

From the top of the dunes, Abby could see that the ocean was quite rough. The waves reared high, like frightened horses, showing white manes of foam before crashing onto the sand. "Wait for me," she called to Ben again, but her voice was swept away by the wind. She watched him standing before the pounding surf. He looked small and absolutely alone. Imagining him lonely and afraid, she dropped the towels onto the sand and ran to him, only to find a smile of delight on his face.

"Look!" Ben said, and swung his arm out over the water. Sunlight sparkled on the backs of the waves.

"The beautiful sea," she said, and in her mind she heard her own mother's voice singing as she held Abby in her arms:

> *By the sea, by the sea, by the beautiful sea*
> *You and me, you and me, oh how happy we'll be*

Ben stood silent for a moment before asking, "But why?"

"Why what, darling?"

"Why do they call it the beautiful *c*? They should call it a beautiful *o*, 'cause it's an ocean."

Abby laughed. "Right you are. Should we put our toes in the beautiful *o*?"

Ben nodded and took her hand. Together, they jumped over the edge of a wave, and landed ankle-deep in the water. Abby squealed. "It's cold!"

"Not for me," Ben chortled.

They stood together, their feet sinking into the sand as

each wave tugged around their ankles before retreating from the shore. Abby felt the sun beating down on her shoulders. Suddenly the water looked cool and inviting. "What do you say, big guy?" she asked her son. "Want to go for a swim?"

"Sure!"

Jack watched his daughter move restlessly about the apartment, flitting like a moth from room to room. She was not the child she used to be—that was for sure. He didn't know if it was the drugs, or the so-called therapy, or the beginning of adolescence, or what, but there was a certain lack of respect in her tone, a snooty little tilt in her chin, that he did not find at all attractive. Maybe that was how kids were allowed to behave in the hospital, but here at home the rules were different, and if Miranda had forgotten that, she would just have to be reminded, because he was sure as hell not going to be treated like that. No way.

"Miranda!" he called, and was pleased when she stood before him.

"Yes, Daddy?"

"I'm going to make dinner, and I want you to take a shower. Wash some of that hospital filth off of yourself before we eat."

"All right."

Jack felt himself relax. The kid was just excited to be home. She was still his little girl, after all. He drew her to him and squeezed her close, then let her go and ruffled her hair. "I'm making lemon chicken," he said. "Your favorite. Bet they didn't feed you that in the hospital, huh?"

She shook her head no, and walked away.

★   ★   ★

Abby hoisted Ben into her arms, above the churning water. He laughed as the spray hit his back. "It tickles!"

She felt strong and confident. She remembered swimming here with her father, feeling safe in his arms as he held her up over the waves. *Don't worry,* he had told her. *No matter how rough it gets close to shore, it's always calm beyond the waves.* She squeezed Ben close and stepped out into the surf.

The food is hot and good, and the metal fork feels heavy in her hand. Outside her ears, her father's voice flows like a river, deep and slow. She is used to voices rushing like a stream, high and fast as they crash over rocks and trickle into pools. *Tell you what. Tomorrow, we'll get back into our old routine. Of course, you're probably way behind, but you'll catch up quick. We'll get you off those drugs they doped you up with and your brain will work as good as new. You'll see. After dinner we can read if you want. We haven't done that in a long time. Remember the book we were reading? Do you? Well, do you? Miranda! Will you answer me, please?*

The words flow by outside, but in her mind she is with Freddy and Natalie and Dr. Cohen, too, and suddenly she is filled with longing, her soul like an outstretched hand begging for food. Her father is silent. She looks up to see him watching her, waiting for her to speak. She returns his gaze. "Well?" he asks again.

"I don't want to stay here," she says. "I want to go back."

★   ★   ★

With practiced timing, Abby waited until each wave broke in front of her before she rushed up to meet the next. "Never be afraid of the waves," she told Ben, who clung, half terrified, half excited, to her neck. "You need to run right to them. If you do, they'll lift you up and over, just like this, nice and gentle. It's only if you're afraid and hang back that they'll clobber you over the noggin."

Ben laughed. "I want them to clobber me over my noggin."

"Now watch out," Abby said. "You never turn your back on the ocean." Ben was growing heavy in her arms. Waist-deep in the water, Abby could tell that the waves were more powerful than she had thought. "Maybe we should head back," she said.

"Mom! You said we could go swimming. You promised."

"All right." She scanned the waves, waiting for her chance to plunge ahead. Down the beach, a group of five or six young men in wet suits were sitting on their surfboards, bobbing up and down on the waves like a flock of overgrown seagulls. Abby wondered briefly whether they would be able to rescue her if she got into trouble, and decided that she was probably on her own. She was almost there anyway. Only two or three more waves, and she'd be out past the breakers and into the calmer water. She snuggled her son against her side. "Hang on tight," she said. " 'Cause here we go."

A wave crested before her. She lifted him over her

head as she remembered her father doing with her, hoping that she could keep Ben's head above the water even if she was submerged, but the power of the wave tore him out of her grasp. "Ben!" she screamed, gulping seawater. He was gone.

He lunged for her, grabbing her around the throat with one hand while the other struck her across her face. "You *what?*"

Miranda fell to the ground. A piece of half-chewed chicken fell from her mouth. Jack straddled her, hand poised to strike. Let her say it again, just one more time. The god-damned bitch—who the hell did she think she was, anyway? All that work he had put in, all those years, and she had turned out just like her mother, after all. Her mouth was moving without sound. "C'mon," he goaded. "Tell me. Maybe I didn't hear right. Tell me again what you *want*, little girl. Daddy needs to know what you *want*."

When it came, the voice was hoarse yet hard, with no hint of fearful tears. "I want my mommy."

He slapped her hard across the face. "You stupid girl. You don't have a mommy. Don't you know that? You never had a mommy. You've got me."

Lying beneath him, she laughed and the world exploded before his eyes. With a sweet release of feeling he slammed his fist over and over into her soft and yielding flesh. She was a bad girl. He needed to teach her a lesson. Relentlessly he pounded his fists against her until at last he heard her cry, as thin and high as an infant's wail. And then, in horror, he stopped.

★   ★   ★

Panicked, Abby grabbed blindly through the foam. Like Sarah he had gone; she would never find him. "Ben!" She would die here, too, better that than lose another child. "Ben!" she screamed again, beating the waves in a frenzy. At last her flailing hand felt flesh and she grabbed on tight and pulled him toward her. She could feel the entire power of the ocean pulling him from her.

"No!" She kept her grip and yanked his head into the air. Her toes thrashed in the water, reaching for the sand, but in the swell of the wave the water was over her head. Ben was crying now, sobbing that he was frightened and wanted to go back. "It's okay," she soothed. "I've got you. It's going to be all right."

And then, suddenly, it was all right. They had made it. The water receded and her feet touched bottom, anchoring her. Behind her, the waves continued to crash against the beach, but where they stood it was miraculously calm. "See?" she told him through her own tears. "We're beyond the waves. We're safe." She rubbed his back, comforting him, comforting them both. "We made it. Look. See how gentle the waves are here?" Slowly, he lifted his face from her neck and faced the sea. A small swell lifted them gently up and then set them gently down again. "You see?" she said again. "We can go up and over, up and over. There's nothing to be afraid of here."

The waves cradled them, rocking them where they stood. Slowly, Ben's grip loosened and Abby felt his body relax, along with her own. "Up and over," he repeated dutifully. His hair against her neck was wet as seaweed.

★   ★   ★

Miranda lies still on the floor, feeling nothing. Far away, she can hear her father's heavy breathing, and the slap of skin against skin. At last he stops and cradles her against him, his sweat and tears falling on her flesh like rain. And then he is gone. She hears the door slam shut behind him, and she lies there, alone. She waits for a long time in the silence, listening for her father. In the silence, her body returns to her and she is covered in pain, but the ache inside is gone. *I want my mommy,* she thinks again, and walks slowly toward the door.

Abby felt strong hands grab her from behind and turned to see Michael's sleek head pop out of the water.

"Hi, there!" she said gratefully as he took Ben from her.

"Just call me Mr. Shark." He nibbled Ben's ear. "Having fun?"

Ben shook his head. "Me and Mommy almost got drownded."

"We did not."

"Uh-huh. There was a big wave and it clobbered me on the noggin, but Mommy saved me and then we were beyond the waves." He paused, considering. "It's funner now."

Abby looked at Michael. "It wasn't that dramatic, I assure you." Really, they had never been in much danger; the waves weren't that rough. But she remembered the fear of losing Ben like a flash of lightning illuminating her need. If the danger had never been real, the love surely was. He was laughing now, paddling through the water in his father's strong arms. She grabbed her husband around his neck and kissed his stubbled cheek, feeling glad that he had joined them in the water, and would be there to help them back to shore.

Epilogue

I t was a shock to come back after vacation. As Abby
stepped off the elevator and into the fetid air of Tower
Ten, she became acutely aware that she had not wanted to
return. Memories of salt air and fresh ocean breezes were
clouded by smells of ammonia, dried urine, and burned
toast. Six of the old kids had left the unit during her absence
and six new bodies shuffled aimlessly down the hall, yet it
seemed that nothing at all had changed. What was the point,
anyway? There was never time to really cure. Just buff them
up and turf them to some halfway house somewhere or to
a crazy, chaotic family, where they would just fall apart
again.

She missed Miranda; perhaps this gloom was no
more than that. Tower Ten seemed lifeless without her. Yet
Abby had gone when Miranda needed her most. It was
her fault, really, that Jack had won. If only she hadn't gone
away. Then Michael's face rose luminous in her mind. She
had gone, and come back whole. It was not Miranda who
filled her now but her family, present and future. She had

told Michael only that morning that her period was late. Inside herself, she felt the familiar ache of a new life growing inside her, easing older pains. But it was hard to give up, to admit that, once again, she had been powerless to cure.

The door clicked shut behind her, locking her onto the unit. In the nurses' station, behind the glass, she saw Laurie greet her with a wave. "Abby! Welcome back," she said. "You'll never guess who wants to see you." In a rush, Laurie told her of the beating and its aftermath, how Miranda had found her way to a policeman and then to St. Ann's, where she was now slowly healing on the seventh floor. "She wants to see you," Laurie told Abby. "That's all she'll say, really. That she wants to see you."

Unable to wait for more, Abby turned her key in the lock and ran back to the elevator. *He'll never get her back now,* she thought. *She's really free.* The elevator came and she stepped inside. *And she wants to see me.* For if Miranda could want even this small thing, then she could learn to want the world: the ocean, the sky, all the grains of sand on a beach, and someone to love.

She would be there soon. As she stepped out of the elevator, Abby felt a wave of nausea wash over her. Morning sickness, a love song. Once you let yourself want, she thought, there was always the chance that you might get. She smiled, knowing that the baby just beginning to grow inside was already struggling to assert its self in opposition to hers. A new life, growing safe within her like a seed taking root in the soil. Her stomach clenched with the ache of desire, and she hugged her new-made baby in her mind, then opened her arms wide to take in Miranda, Ben, Michael, and even Sarah, lifting them with her love and then gently letting go, believing they'd never leave.

Elizabeth Marek, a practicing psychologist, is the author of one previous work of nonfiction, *The Children at Santa Clara*. She lives with her husband, two children, one dog, and one rabbit in Westchester County, New York, but looks forward all year to her summer retreats on Martha's Vineyard.

Beyond the Waves

ELIZABETH MAREK

This Conversation Guide is intended to enrich the
individual reading experience, as well as encourage us
to explore these topics together—because books,
and life, are meant for sharing.

A CONVERSATION
WITH ELIZABETH MAREK

Q. *Like Abby, the main character in the novel, you are a psychologist and a mother. Is this an autobiographical work?*

A. Not in any literal sense. I have never worked with a patient like Miranda, never suffered the death of a child, and have a relationship with my husband very different from the one portrayed in the book. But of course, all fiction is autobiographical to some extent. In trying to imagine what Abby might have felt after the death of her daughter, Sarah, I called upon feelings I had when my son was critically ill, as well as the grief I experienced following the death of my mother. Those experiences taught me that recovering from grief is a long-term process that can be quite isolating. It is certainly true that this society frowns upon prolonged mourning. After six months, there is a pressure to "snap out of it" and resume being the person you were before the tragedy. But grief changes you, and the person you were before may no longer exist. I see Abby as struggling to come to terms with her new identity, and to help her family accept the person she is as different from the person she was. Since that struggle was a central piece of my own young adulthood, I suppose you could say that in some sense the novel is emotionally autobiographical.

Q. Miranda and her father are such strange characters, and their relationship is very disturbing. What inspired you to write about them?

A. I was watching a production of Shakespeare's *The Tempest,* and I became fascinated with the idea of a parent loving a child so much that he (or she) would attempt to create a completely safe and controlled world, in which no physical or emotional harm could occur. After I had my children, and especially after my first child became so ill, that fantasy took on even more weight for me. I think all parents, on some level, would love to seal their child in a protective bubble. Yet of course the implications for the child would be devastating. A good parent knows that she needs to allow her children the freedom to make mistakes, even to get hurt. It's the hardest thing we do as parents, really. My parents had a saying: "Hold them close and then let them go." But Jack couldn't do that. In the end, his needs—for Miranda to be safe, for her to love him, for her to stay *his*—made it impossible for him to see or accept her needs.

Q. As a psychologist, you must come in contact with a lot of interesting personalities. How does being a psychologist inform your writing? Is it helpful?

A. I don't think that being a psychologist has made me a better writer. If anything, I think it's possible that being a writer has made me a better psychologist! I think that both professions require a rich imagination. They are both concerned with trying to put yourself in another person's skin, to understand people's actions in the context of their motivations and emotions. And of course, both writing and psychology are at some level about stories. The best part of being a psychologist, for me, is hearing the stories that people create out of their lives.

Q. What books or authors do you feel have had an influence on your writing? Whom do you read for fun?

A. I love to read books with rich characters and beautiful language. I think William Faulkner's use of stream of consciousness and internal monologues had a profound impact on my own writing, particularly *The Sound and the Fury*. I first read that in high school, and remember being absolutely amazed by the way that he could capture and make immediate and real the inchoate thoughts and emotions of a nonverbal "idiot." I thought of that often as I tried to capture Miranda's internal experience in *Beyond the Waves*. Similarly, I love the way Virginia Woolf conveys the different voices of her characters in *Mrs. Dalloway* and *To the Lighthouse*. In terms of contemporary fiction, I greatly enjoyed *The Life of Pi,* by Yann Martel, and the idea that we all need to make stories from the stuff our lives are made of; our lives would be unbearable otherwise.

Q. Was writing always something you knew you wanted to do?

A. I have always loved to write. When I was a kid, I wanted to be a writer the way that other kids want to be baseball players or rock stars.

Q. What are you writing now?

A. Right now, I'm working on a nonfiction book called *Children Who Won't*. It's a parenting guide for parents with oppositional or "difficult" children. In case my children read this, I will assure you that *this* book is not autobiographical, either. My kids are actually pretty good most of the time.

QUESTIONS
FOR DISCUSSION

1. Is Abby a good mother?

2. Abby and Jack parent their children in very different ways. Do you see any similarities between them? If Abby could have kept Sarah safe by secluding her, as Jack secluded Miranda, do you think she would have done so?

3. What do you think about Abby's relationship with Tom? Would your feelings be different if she had allowed herself to become involved in a full-blown affair with him?

4. Can you relate to the strains in Abby's marriage to Michael? Is she a good wife? Is he a good husband?

5. Do you like Abby? Do you think that you would be friends with her?

6. In the book, it has been two years since Abby's daughter's death. Do you think that Abby's feelings—her grief and numbness—are reasonable after that length of time? Does it seem typical? Understandable?

7. Did any of the characters in the novel do anything that really surprised you?

8. What are the different meanings, positive and negative, that the ocean has for Abby?

9. Which character changes the most in the course of the novel?

10. What do you think will happen to Abby after the book ends? To Miranda? To Jack?